CRASH

A new novel from this master story-teller

One beautiful Scottish spring day, Julian Custer comes across the devastating scene of a very recent car crash. Only the passenger has survived: Delia Barrow is confused and badly injured; her name is all she can remember. It seems that Julian is all Delia has. Luckily, Julian is a solicitor, and so begins a voyage of discovery as they try to discover the identity of the passengers in the other vehicle...

CRASH

Gerald Hammond

Severn House Large Print
London & New York

This first large print edition published 2010
in Great Britain and the USA by
SEVERN HOUSE PUBLISHERS LTD of
9-15 High Street, Sutton, Surrey, SM1 1DF.
First world regular print edition published 2008 by
Severn House Publishers Ltd., London and New York.

British Library Cataloguing in Publication Data

Hammond, Gerald, 1926-
  Crash.
  1. Traffic accident investigation--Fiction. 2. Detective
  and mystery stories. 3. Large type books.
  I. Title
  823.9'14-dc22

ISBN-13: 978-0-7278-7844-1

Printed and bound in Great Britain by
MPG Books Ltd, Bodmin, Cornwall.

One

It was too beautiful a day for death and destruction. Spring was becoming summer, a time that often brings the best weather of the year to Scotland; and an unusual heat-wave held sway.

The grey saloon car was crumpled against the stone wall. The dark marks of its slide across the grass were aligned with fainter braking and skid-marks on the tarmac. From these it appeared that the car had been travelling north, in the general direction of John O'Groats, some 70-odd miles further on. A long break between the two sets of marks suggested that the car had taken a leap from the kerb. Julian Custer brought his estate car to a hasty halt on the grass verge and twisted to get his long legs out. Somebody needed help and it was in his nature to give it. Behind him, Grace Campbell also stopped her Mondeo.

The accident was very recent – indeed, thinking back, Julian thought that he might have heard it only seconds ago as he neared the last bend before the junction. One front wheel, caught off the ground, was still turning. The car was making the hissing, tinkling sounds that a hot car makes after a smash. The passenger's door was open and a young woman had been thrown out when they jumped the kerb, some yards before the impact. Her attitude was such that he was sure that she had suffered broken bones. Her clothes were dishevelled but she was safe where she was for the moment. He could hear Grace speaking calmly and clearly on her mobile, demanding connection to emergency services.

But there was a figure in the driving seat in far more need of rescue than the woman on the grass verge. A man, not very old – or at least he seemed to have a full head of hair – was slumped in the driver's seat, supported by the inflated airbag. It seemed that the airbag might not have been sufficient to save him, because there was blood on his face and his head was unpleasantly twisted to the side. But the smell of petrol was dominating

6

the scene. The tank, he thought, had been holed when they jumped the kerb. He detoured round the steady trickle of fuel that was running part-way towards the road before sinking into the turf. The sickening smell of fuel alone nearly turned him back.

Given another minute, he might have saved the driver or the driver's body. Given only a few more seconds, he would have run into the flames. After such an impact there were bound to be electrical faults to be found by the petrol that was being vaporized by the hot exhaust. With a soft explosion, the fuel on the ground ignited. It was followed by a fireball such as he had thought to be the copyright of the film industry. In deference to the fine weather, Julian had been driving in a short-sleeved shirt and without a jacket. He felt the hair sizzle on his arms as he backed out of danger. Black smoke was swirling up, casting a shadow over the scene.

For a living driver trapped in the inferno he might have tried, despite the certainty of serious burns to himself. With the driver so evidently past saving, the woman had priority. She was clear of the flames but exposed to the radiant heat. Grace was already pulling the woman clear by her right arm.

Julian hurried to help. 'Careful,' Grace said. 'Her left leg's broken and her left arm seems to be injured. Take her under the armpit.' They drew her well clear and laid her gently back down. 'Leave her. We could be doing more harm than good.'

Knowing Grace to be a very well qualified physiotherapist, Julian deferred. He straightened up. His heart began to slow down from its nervous gallop but his mouth was very dry. His forearms were stinging. 'Who did you call?' he asked her.

'Ambulance and fire brigade.'

'You'd better call the police as well. There's a dead driver.'

While Grace made further use of her cellphone, he turned his attention to the traffic. The lack of other vehicles, at least northbound, was soon explained by the arrival of a slow and heavy articulated lorry followed, with varying degrees of patience, by a short tailback. The lorry driver pulled up and jumped down carrying a heavy fire extinguisher. His vehicle partly screened the wreck from view. The few passing drivers slowed and stared but evidently decided to move on before the police arrived and closed the road. The lorry driver sprayed foam over and into the car.

The woman on the grass began to stir. 'Oh God,' she said. 'Oh God, Oh God, Oh God.'

'Do you know your own name?' Grace asked. She stooped and pulled down the girl's skirt, a womanly gesture towards modesty.

'Delia. Delia Barrow. My leg hurts.' There was a faint trace of what might have been a cockney accent.

'What happened, Delia?'

There was a long pause. 'Don't remember.' She was younger than Julian had thought at first – very late teens or early twenties. She had a healthy-looking tan and without make-up she still managed to present a likeable face without being sexually appealing.

The emergency services only had to come the few miles from Dornoch. They arrived almost together within a few minutes and each went into a well-drilled routine. The fire officers added to the foam. The flames, which had been reduced to occasional spurts by the attention of the lorry driver, were replaced by more smoke and the stinks of burnt paint and plastic. There was another smell that Julian tried hard not to identify.

One paramedic hurried to the burnt car but he turned back after one long look. Both paramedics stooped over Delia Barrow. The lone traffic officer, after setting out a warning sign and some cones, drew Julian aside and produced his incident book and a ballpoint pen. He rested the book on the roof of Julian's car.

Julian gave his name, his address and his occupation – solicitor. 'I didn't see the crash,' he said. 'Mrs Campbell was taking her car for its service and MOT and I had offered to run her home again.'

'But you were first on the scene?'

'I suppose so. We seemed to have arrived just after it happened.'

They were interrupted. The paramedics had loaded Ms Barrow into the ambulance. One of them approached Julian. 'You too,' he said.

'What do you mean?'

'Your arms are burnt. You'd better come in to Raigmore. They have a better burns unit there than the locals can provide and they can put the young lady through the scanner.'

The policeman moved and stooped. 'He's right,' he said. 'I couldn't see it because you were facing me but you'd better get that seen to. I'll get a statement from your wife.'

His arms had only been stinging, As soon as he was told that they were burnt, the backs or undersides, whichever way you wanted to look at it, began to hurt. He took refuge in an irrelevancy. 'I don't have a wife. Mrs Campbell's my next-door neighbour.'

Grace Campbell turned away from the ambulance. She was tall and fair-haired and although she was still in her early thirties she could only be considered stately. 'Grace,' Julian said, 'I'll have to go in with the ambulance and get some scorching attended to. Will you get somebody to collect my car?'

Grace looked at his forearms. 'Yes, of course I will. You'd better go. The sooner those are dealt with the better.'

'I'm going.' But Julian had a dislike of hospitals and instinct told him that once he was committed to the ambulance he would be enmeshed in the machinery of diagnosis and surgery. His mind, seeking escape, looked for a change of subject and found it. He was quite unaware of the forces he would be setting in motion. 'My camera's in my car, on the back seat. I suggest you take a shot of those skid-marks.'

'I will. Now go.'

Julian turned and made his way to the ambulance. One of the paramedics moved as if to take his arm and then thought better of it.

In the ambulance, the other ambulance man was finishing the tasks of rendering Ms Barrow relatively comfortable and stable. Both men tutted over Julian's burns. 'You're lucky,' one said. He turned out later to be the driver. 'They're not all the way through the skin.' He began very gently to smear a greasy substance over Julian's burns. His partner laid cling film over the top. Julian made an enquiring noise. 'It's the air passing over a burn that makes it hurt,' the driver explained. Julian immediately felt a lessening of the pain. He never decided whether this was due to the power of suggestion.

The driver removed to the driving seat and spoke over the radio. The ambulance moved off. The other man seated himself beside Julian. 'Would you rather lie flat?' he asked.

Lying flat, his forearms would have to rest on something. Sitting up, he could keep them out of harm's way. 'I'm fine here,' Julian said.

'That's good. That jump seat is just murder

on the coccyx.'

They travelled for some distance in silence. Julian could see familiar landmarks as they passed. He was suddenly aware of a brown eye regarding him. The other was half hidden by a pink-tinged nose. Her hair, somewhere between brown and blonde, had managed to remain almost tidy. 'You're not my brother,' she said huskily. 'Are you?' she added.

'No, I'm not.'

She drifted off to sleep, or fell into a coma – he did not feel qualified to judge. They had crossed the Cromarty Firth when the eye flicked open again. 'Where's Ally?' she asked.

'Is Ally your brother?'

'Yes. He's Aloysius really, but he hates being called that. I call him Ally. Ally Barrow. Not much better.'

If she still shared her surname with her brother it seemed unlikely that there was a husband to be informed. Her left hand was hidden in the plastic splint. The eye had closed again. It was later and they were near Inverness when it opened again – they were passing the high arches of the bridge over the Moray Firth. The sunlight was dancing on the water and there were gulls wheeling overhead.

'Where is Ally? Is he all right? There was a crash, wasn't there?' Her voice was stronger and he was still sure that he could detect a trace of an accent, possibly Australian.

'Yes,' he said. 'There was a crash. Was your brother driving?'

'Probably. I don't remember. We took it in turns. Is this an ambulance? If I'm in an ambulance, why isn't he? Was he not hurt? He's usually lucky.'

Julian wanted to say *Not this time* but he accepted that breaking bad news was not his responsibility. 'You were thrown out of the car.'

After a moment she seemed to accept that as sufficient answer. 'Who are you?' she asked.

'My name's Julian Custer.'

The paramedic only had snatches of overheard discussion to go by, so his appreciation of the story was incomplete. 'This gentleman got burnt trying to save–'. He broke off, suddenly aware that he was about to break the news. He snatched at a change of subject. 'He's a solicitor, a lawyer.'

Her mind was alert enough to see the implications. 'Ally's dead, isn't he?'

The question put Julian in a quandary.

Medical practice is to keep bad news away from the patient for as long as possible but a lawyer learns to bring his clients to confrontation with disaster before it can get worse. This time, professional habit won. 'I'm afraid so.'

She seemed to take the tidings bravely, just closing her eyes. They snapped open again after a minute or so. 'I'm not thinking clearly,' she said. 'Not taking it in. Have I been given something?'

'Just a painkiller,' the paramedic said.

'That's what's doing it. Tell me again, later.' She seemed to fall asleep after that.

Back at the accident site the lorry driver – a fat and fussy man with a luxuriant moustache – made a short statement and was allowed to go on his way. Grace retrieved Julian's camera. 'Damn!' she said. 'It's a digital. I've never used one of these.'

'I have one just like it,' said the officer.

Grace handed over the camera. 'All right,' she said. 'You use it.'

'This is a fatal accident.' He glanced unhappily at the burnt car. 'All the technical support will be here soon.'

Grace had never been one to hesitate in the

face of fatuous arguments. 'Listen,' she said firmly. 'Those tyre-marks tell a story but they may or may not outlast this traffic or a shower of rain. Let's take the photographs first and argue afterwards.'

'That seems reasonable.' The officer switched on the camera and checked the position of the mode dial.

'Try to take them against the light,' Grace told him. 'That way they'll show up more clearly.'

The officer was prepared to bristle at being advised – almost ordered – by a member of the public, but when he looked he found that she was quite correct. There was a lull in the traffic. He zoomed out the lens and took a series of shots. They checked them in the monitor and saw that the tyre-marks showed up quite clearly. From the distance came the sound of a police vehicle in a hurry.

'Very observant of you, if I may say so,' he said quickly. 'But they may have been made at quite different times.'

Grace nodded. 'Obviously. But they may not.'

'No. It looks very much as if they happened together. We'll see what the boss says. Do you mind if...?' His voice tailed away.

'Go ahead,' Grace said. 'Help yourself to any credit that's going. How soon can I get away?'

The officer shrugged.

Grace sat in her car and used her cellphone to call the garage, her husband and then the patient who was expecting her. To each, she gave a very brief explanation of the delay. While she was speaking, a vehicle in police livery drew up. Two men went straight to the burnt car. The third, a uniformed sergeant, spoke with the constable.

'On the face of it,' the traffic constable said, 'it looks like a simple traffic accident. Attention wandering, driver distracted, an animal in the road or whatever. That may be just what happened. Unfortunately there were no witnesses. The gentleman who was first on the scene was slightly burnt and he went in to Raigmore in the ambulance with the passenger from the crashed car. The lady was following him. Neither of them saw the crash, only the aftermath.'

The sergeant was not interested in witnesses who had seen nothing. 'You said "On the face of it",' he pointed out. 'Off the face of it, what?'

'You can still make out the tyre-tracks on

the road. The turf's very dry and the tyre-marks may fade away quickly, but I borrow-ed a camera and photographed them and the ones on the road in case the traffic rubs them away.' He led his superior towards the crashed car but turned aside to the road verge. 'You can see where he hit the grass, so these are the tracks of this car. You can see where they suddenly turn aside, hit the kerb and jump on to the grass. Up to the point where they turn aside there are no tracks, so the vehicle was travelling on a normal course and in a normal manner. Braking begins at that point.'

'Steering failure, you think?'

'Perhaps, Sarge. But there is another set of tracks, of a wider vehicle than the first car. They come out of the road past Cairnfauld and turn sharp left. From the point where they leave that road they are dark and distinct, which suggests heavy braking. That vehicle should have made its turn without crossing the central line at all. But the tracks cross the centre-line of the A9 just where the first vehicle swerves and they return to their own side of the road and fade away. To me, that suggests a vehicle travelling too fast to make the turn without drifting across the road. The driver of the car had to take evasive action that resulted in the crash.'

The sergeant took another look at the tracks and turned to look again at the crashed car. He hated to admit that his subordinate had beaten him to the truth. On the other hand, the younger man had been on the scene for much longer. 'Well done, laddie,' he said. 'But you're mistaken on one point.' Magnanimously, he decided to overlook the fact that the absence of witnesses had been his own observation. 'We do have witnesses.'

'We do, Sarge?'

'We do. First, the lady passenger. She's still alive and expected to remain so?'

'I believe so, Sarge.'

'Then there is the couple who arrived on the scene first. They seem to have been coming from the direction of Inverness, which is the direction in which this other vehicle drove off. It must have passed them. We will ask this lady. She must have seen it.'

But Grace, when questioned, proved to be a disappointment. She had been following Julian and had little recollection of anything other than the back of his estate car. 'It's no good badgering me,' she said at last. 'I have

19

a vague recollection of something that may or may not have been a white van, unless you planted that idea in my head. If you force the issue, you'll only be making me dig in my subconscious for a description that may be from memory or from imagination, I'd have no way of knowing. Try Julian, or the woman who was thrown out of the car. You'll find them both in Raigmore Hospital, Inverness.'

'We will get an officer from Inverness to take statements,' said the sergeant.

Two

Julian Custer, while protesting that he was perfectly capable of walking, was firmly ordered into a wheelchair. This, he was assured, was in case shock should cause him suddenly to faint, but he suspected that the reason was more that a patient afoot might wander anywhere, even into the sacred precincts of the surgeons' changing rooms. The movements of a patient in a wheelchair are more easily predicted and controlled than those of one who is still allowed to move at will. Delia Barrow was whisked away almost immediately for X-rays and scanning but Julian was shunted into a cubicle where, after a short and uncomfortable wait, a doctor examined his burns and then left him at the mercy of a pair of nurses.

He was allowed to undress himself and they lent him a hospital dressing gown. The burns were unwrapped, re-anointed, re-wrapped in cling film and treated to bandages over the top ... The nurses worked efficiently but chattered constantly about their outing the previous evening. It was soon clear that a patient was not considered to be a real, sentient being, capable of listening and understanding. The nurses were dealing with one forearm apiece so that Julian could not even put his fingers in his ears.

The doctor returned and repeated the paramedic's comment that he had been lucky. Julian supposed that, in the sense that he had not been fatally fried, that was true but that he would have been much luckier if someone else had got to the accident scene first.

'How is Miss Barrow?' Julian asked. 'The young lady who came in with me?'

The doctor seemed to assume that there was some sort of relationship so that patient confidentiality did not apply. 'Last I heard, she was having a greenstick fracture set. Her left arm's suffered sprains but no bones broken. Nothing serious showed up on the X-rays but we won't be sure for a day or two.'

'That's good. When can I go home?'

'I want to keep you in for twenty-four hours or so. Burns are very subject to infections. If you're all right tomorrow, you can go home.'

Julian knew that he was unjustifiably touchy about people who assumed authority that they didn't have. He was tempted to point out that he could go home any time he liked but that he was prepared to accept contrary advice on this one occasion. However, he could recognize the sense in the advice and also he made a point of never antagonizing policemen, dentists, doctors, judges or bank managers. He meekly allowed himself to be trundled up to a ward where the sister found him a pair of pyjamas (he suspected that the original owner might have died on the operating table) and, on production of the necessary coins, allowed him to phone Grace's number and pass on the latest news. Grace would have regaled him with a lengthy report of the police activities following his departure, but Julian pointed out that he had limited cash with him and that calls from a hospital pay phone to a mobile cost the earth. Grace promised to phone in the morning for tidings.

There were eight beds on the ward and the other seven occupants had already digested the morning papers and were prepared to pass them on. Four different dailies and an angling magazine were represented and Julian was preparing to pass the rest of the day in reading. A visit by a traffic policeman from Inverness passed a few minutes but Julian was unable to give him any real facts about the smash.

However, soon after the evening meal – quite a passable meal, hospital meals had improved since he had had his appendix removed – a lady in a variant of the nurses' uniform appeared at his bedside. He decided that she was either very junior or very senior and he was not too worried as to which. 'Are you the gentleman who came in with Miss

Barrow?' she asked.

Julian said that he was. 'How is she doing?' he asked.

'As well as can be expected,' she said. Before Julian could object to the uninformative reply she went on, 'Miss Barrow wants a word with you and she won't settle until she gets it. If you're agreeable I can fetch a porter with a wheelchair.'

Julian had no particular wish to comfort the bereaved but it would be a break in the endless monotony of hospital life. He knew too well how time would begin to drag. He said that he could walk perfectly well, thank you. That was before he discovered that the slippers loaned to him were several sizes too large, but he had a profound dislike of being seen to change his mind, even over something so trivial. He managed somehow with a comical, waddling gait. He had already discovered that Raigmore did not have a specialist burns unit – burns, apparently, came under Dermatology. He was led to a lift and thence to what was evidently a female orthopaedic ward. He thought that, no matter what the variations of shape and colour, or even in the dark, a hospital could never be mistaken for anything but a hospital. The smells and sounds alone were too distinctive.

Delia Barrow lay prone. Apart from a small cut with two stitches, her face was unmarked. Despite the tan, her skin was good so that any lack of make-up was immaterial. Somebody had even made an attempt to tidy her hair again, but in no particular style. The result was an appearance suggesting a happy, outdoor and, even in a hospital bed, healthy girl, not beautiful, not even more than slightly pretty, but piquant and unmistakably feminine. Her expression was serious although her cast of features suggested someone who could laugh and even love wholeheartedly and who had come to bereavement almost as a stranger.

Her left arm and leg were each in some kind of moulded splint but at least no traction had been considered necessary. Julian took the chair beside the bed and a curtain was drawn round to form a cubicle. It gave both Delia and him and the ladies on the ward privacy from view but he was aware that every word spoken would be audible to those other ladies. Her eyes had been open, staring dully towards the ceiling, but she brought them down. She seemed to have to make an effort to focus on him.

He was seated to her right, so she had no difficulty in holding out that hand. He took it, which she seemed to expect and to find comforting. 'Thank you for coming,' she said softly. 'I couldn't think of anyone else. I don't know anybody in Britain. Nobody at all.'

'That's all right. How do you feel?'

'A bit sore, but not too bad. I guess they've got me pretty well doped up. I feel kind of woozy. But they've done a good job on me.'

'That's good. What do you remember?'

'Not a lot. I've got a lump like half an apple on my head. I remember coming to in the ambulance, more or less. There's already been a policeman from Inverness, asking me what I remember from just before the smash. I had to tell him I remember Ally driving us over that big suspension bridge north of Inverness and after that nothing. I was looking down at the map just before it happened. I said that they'd better try you or your wife.'

'I don't have a wife,' Julian said.

'Is that so? Somebody – the ambulance driver, I think – said that there was a lady with you. They tell me that my memory may or may not come back to me.' She paused. He saw her hands whiten as she clasped them together. She was bracing herself for an effort of courage. 'Listen, do I remember you telling me that Ally was killed?'

'I'm afraid so.'

'I didn't take it in at the time and that cop didn't know, or said he didn't. And you got burnt trying to pull him out?'

'Sort of. I didn't get very close and I think it was already too late.'

'It was brave of you all the same. Do you mind if we're quiet for a minute?'

'Of course not,' he said.

They were silent for several minutes. When she moved, it was to dab at her eyes with a tissue. 'Let's leave it there for now,' she said. 'I'll do my grieving in my own time.'

'That's sensible. And very brave.' He wondered about a change of subject. 'Are you Australian?'

She smiled faintly. 'Do I sound Strine? No, I'm from New Zealand, a Kiwi, except that I was born not far from here. The family went out there when I was three. Listen, do I remember somebody saying that you're a lawyer? A solicitor?'

'That's right.'

'Well, I got a real problem and maybe you can help. Can I tell you about it?'

Julian Custer had just finished work on a major arbitration. He was having a long break before starting work in a new partnership in Tain and he was settling in to a house in a country setting and struggling to get the house and garden how he wanted them. For the moment, he had no staff, no facilities, not even any stationery. He had no wish to be saddled with a private client. But for the moment he was faced with a period of hospital-induced boredom. If it helped her, he would listen and then perhaps suggest the name of a more suitable representative.

'Go ahead,' he said.

'Was anything saved from the car? Any luggage?'

'I think it very unlikely.'

'Crikey! Well, here's the way of it. I guess the best way would be to tell it in chronological order. Otherwise we'll be jumping forwards and back again. My grandad was a sheep farmer up this way, but the way things were at the time, with rents and all, there was hardly a living in it. The whole family upped and went to New Zealand. Grandad and my dad both worked for a sheep farmer on South Island and when the owner died they bought the place with the help of the bank. Grandad died when I was ten but my father was killed in an accident with an ORV just last year. The farm had been doing well and the bank was just about paid off.

'Ally and I inherited the place and the stock jointly. I had a fiancé at that time though nothing came of it – he turned out to be a louse who was off like a rocket when a girl with more money showed up – but Dad seems to have assumed that Ally would have more need of an inheritance than I would, so he split it two-thirds to Ally and one-third to me. That was fair enough – I had no complaints. We went on farming it. We were happy but Ally had fond memories of Scotland. He wanted to come back here and I was quite willing to go with him.'

'You'll be facing a cold climate here,' Julian said.

Even while lying flat, Delia managed to convey an impression of bridling. When severe weather is under discussion, most natives are eager to endorse their home weather as being worse than anybody else's.

'South Island is well down in the Roaring Forties, almost into the Fifties.'

'We're further from the Equator than that.'

'Do you have glaciers?'

He cast his mind back to the rolling countryside, heather-clad hills and barren mountains, sculpted by glaciers but left to the mercy of frost and snowfall for more years than he could imagine. He had to smile. 'Not any longer.'

'There you are, then. And South Island doesn't sit in a Gulf Stream. I think we could have faced it. Then, out of the blue, we had an offer from a neighbour, to buy the place and stock at valuation.' Her brown eyes opened wide. 'My God ... What's your name? I forgot to ask.'

'Julian Custer.'

'May I call you Julian?'

'Please do.'

'Then please call me Delia. Or Dell for preference. That's what Ally always calls ... called me. I still can't get used to the idea that he'll never call me that again.' She sniffed. 'My God, Julian, we had no idea how values had been shooting up. It was our chance and too good to pass up.

'Ally had been watching the trade papers

and he saw that the Earl of Caithness was advertising for a farm manager to improve the breeding of thousands and thousands of hill sheep. He applied and got the job. We sold everything and came away. We were driving north to take up the post when, I suppose, some silly bugger forced us off the road.'

'Nobody saw another car,' Julian said carefully. 'Not that I've heard of yet. But there were some marks in the road suggesting that somebody came out of the road from your right. The police are looking into it.'

She frowned. A frown seemed out of place on a face that was born to be cheerful. 'Ally is ... was much too careful a driver to have a smash all on his own. I won't pretend that he was slow. He didn't hang about, getting in people's way, but he was always in control and aware of every change in the traffic pattern.'

'We'll have to see what the police dig up. What are you going to do now?'

'That's what I wanted to ask you. Unless somebody rescued a satchel of papers out of the car I can't even prove who I am, let alone claim my own bank accounts and be Ally's next of kin. I don't have a passport or a birth

31

certificate. I don't even have a chequebook or any cash. It was all in the car. If I walk out of here, I starve.'

Julian smiled at the quaint concept. 'Not literally. Nobody starves in this country unless they want to. You have an identifiable signature. Do you remember your PIN numbers?'

She thought for a moment. The effort of memory brought another frown. 'Yes,' she said at last.

'Then we can get you some money within a few days. It will take a little time but they'll probably want to keep you in here for at least that long. They complain about a shortage of beds but once they've got you they don't like to let you go.'

The frown was replaced by a smile. Her face, he realized, was well proportioned and appealing. It was still neither beautiful nor even pretty, her features were too individual for that, but when she smiled – in relief, he thought – it was transformed. She could have passed for the stereotypical Girl Next Door. Which, he thought suddenly, she was almost certainly going to be.

'Then you're going to take me on as a client? You have time for me?'

'Yes,' he said. 'I'll take you on. I have plenty of time.' It was time in which he had hoped to make his new house and garden accord with his taste, but if Miss Barrow's affairs took up much of his time perhaps her fees would pay for some professional help. 'I'll phone Grace to bring my camera when she comes to fetch me tomorrow.'

'Is Grace your wife?'

He hid a smile. A woman is always womanly. 'I thought I mentioned that I'm not married. Grace is the lady next door.'

'I guess my memory still isn't working right. And the camera?'

'One of the first things we need is proof of your identity. If you were born in Britain I can get a copy of your birth certificate. With that, we can apply for a replacement passport. For that, I need photographs. Wait a minute. Don't go away.'

She managed to laugh though it was a poor shadow of laughter.

From the nurse's station he cadged a pencil and a small notebook. He seated himself beside her again. 'Let's have every personal detail that you can remember. Where was your passport issued? And your driving licence?'

Her memory of things leading up to the accident might be faulty but her recall of earlier details was sharp and clear. Julian had to remind her to lower her voice when she quoted details about bank accounts and PIN numbers.

Three

Julian passed a restless night on a hospital bed that was rather harder and hotter than he was used to. His burns nagged him until the ward sister gave him a pill. But he ate and enjoyed an adequate breakfast. He had to fret until the doctors came on ward round. It was decided that his burns had escaped infection and that he needed no more treatment than could be provided at his local surgery. He could go home later that day.

Grace had contracted a fondness for Julian. It was either Platonic or maternal, she was uncertain which, but, contacted by phone, she postponed several appointments. She arrived complete with Julian's camera. She insisted on attending the photographic session, which took place in the middle of Delia's ward during visiting hours with Delia in a wheelchair and several patients and a visitor chipping in with advice. As soon as she could be sure that Delia Barrow posed no immediate threat to her neighbour, Grace took over make-up and hairdressing duties. She soon decided that Delia was a very suitable person for Julian.

Delia, after a life spent on a sheep station, was nonplussed to find that several other people considered her appearance to be a matter worthy of serious consideration. Several times, she protested that it was only for a passport photograph, for God's sake, to which Grace retorted that because it would be a passport photograph she would have to live with it for some years to come. Only when the lighting and the background of cubicle curtains seemed satisfactory and the neckline of the hospital gown was concealed by Grace's own scarf did she allow Julian to proceed, and even then insisted on seeing the images on the camera's monitor before passing the results as fit for reproduction.

Delia, it seemed, was faced with the probability of at least a week in hospital. Julian managed to have a private word with her before he left. 'You mustn't mind Grace,' he said. 'She's the bossy type – I suppose as a physiotherapist she has to be – but it's very well meant.'

Delia seemed surprised that the comment had been made at all. 'I could see that. I liked her. And she thinks a whole lot of you. You will stay in touch, won't you?'

He laughed. 'Yes, of course I will. Did you think that I was going to walk out on you?' He had again borrowed pen and paper from the nurses' station. He placed it carefully. 'You can write?'

Delia had recovered some of her spirits. 'We Kiwis are not all illiterate savages. But perhaps you mean can I still write in spite of my injuries? No problem there. My right arm still works.'

'Fine. Write me out an authorization to act on your behalf.' He dictated a wording. 'Now, do you have change for the hospital phone?'

'I don't have any cash,' she reminded him.

He emptied the change from his pocket. 'This should last you for several days. Try not to have to phone me and, if you do have to, here's my card. Call my landline number, not my mobile. Leave a message on my Answerphone if necessary – hospital phones are grossly overpriced and calling a mobile from one of them ... you'd be cheaper hiring a courier with a helicopter. I'll call you regularly. Let me know how your memory's coming back.'

She held out her hand and he had to take it again. 'Thank you,' she said huskily. 'I don't know what I'd have done if you hadn't turned up.'

On his way down to the car, he retained the image of her warm, dry, trusting hand. Nevertheless, he paused and made a note of the small sum that he had advanced to Delia. He could include it in his final account. If it had not been for the accident and her injuries he would have suspected that her story had all the makings of a classic con trick.

Grace was already in the driving seat and had brought the car round to the main exit door beside A and E. That part of the hospital, he thought, had been tacked on to the seven floors of the hospital building and looked like a glorified Portakabin. It was his experience of hospitals that the better architecture went with the best treatment, but whether that was a matter of finance or of staff morale he had no idea.

The car was his. (Her car, she said, had not yet received its test certificate due to the previous day's delays.) Like most men, he hated being driven in his own car but he let her drive – movement of his forearms was still inclined to be tender as the skin was pulled to and fro. She made her way through the hospital's roundabout system and out into Old Perth Road. 'You're taking her on as a client?' she asked.

'That seems to be the general idea.'

In Grace's opinion, Delia might make a satisfactorily submissive girlfriend or even a wife for Julian but she would not be a good client. 'You're going to need your time,' she said.

'You think?'

'I know. She told me that every document she ever had went up in smoke. That alone will take some unscrambling. She's the clinging type and you'll find that she can't do anything for herself. I think that this may be the first time that she's found herself without

38

a male relative to do her thinking for her. Add to it that another vehicle seems to have driven them off the road. You were right about that. I studied the tracks with that traffic officer after you were carried off in the ambulance. I may be able to help a little with that.'

'How's that?' he asked.

'I belong here and although I was away for some time I've been living here again for years. I know people and Stuart, as a depute headmaster, has contact with a lot of pairs of observant eyes and curious voices. I'll see what I can find out. I can't promise anything.'

'No, of course you can't.'

They were silent, each busy with private thoughts, until they neared the Cromarty Firth. Then she said, 'You'd better get Geordie Munro to take over your decorating. He's paid off and at home just now, waiting for the next phase of Canmore House Hotel. I'll speak to him for you, shall I?' Geordie Munro, with his sister Hilda, occupied the third house of the tiny group.

He had not known her for very long but he was regularly irritated by Grace's habit of telling him to do what he had already decided was the way to go. 'I know Geordie quite well, thank you,' Julian said. 'I'll speak to him.' After a pause he added, 'It's a sensible suggestion. Thank you.'

'Don't mention it.'

'Was anything saved at the crash site?'

Grace decided to forgive his momentary abruptness. 'Not a thing,' she said. 'They kept me waiting for what seemed like hours, wanting a statement but not getting around to taking one until they'd studied all the signs. I had plenty of time to watch them examining what was left of the car and sur-roundings. Believe me, the car and its con-tents were incinerated. I'd love to be able to tell you that a briefcase full of passports and bank statements was thrown clear, but I'm afraid it just didn't happen.'

'I didn't suppose that it did,' he said sadly.

They went by the short cut over the hills and came down to the Dornoch Firth not far short of Bonar Bridge. Grace pulled into the front driveway of the house that Julian had bought not many months earlier. It was a pleasing house, the middle one of the three. It was well designed and built – the two do not always go hand in hand. The three houses were well situated, with farmland on both sides and a view over the Firth to the sunlit side of the hills beyond. The hills sheltered the area from the south although it had to be admitted that they would cut off the sun during the winter at certain times of day. The house was very neat and well maintained, but Julian considered the interior decoration hideous and the garden to be unimaginative and somehow reminiscent of the worst sort of municipal park. It was understood locally that Mr and Mrs Sands had kept the house to await their retirement but a single winter had changed their minds for them and they had returned to South Africa. Julian's theory was that they had fled from their own colour schemes rather than face the humiliation of having to order them changed, thereby admitting a series of terrible mistakes. Before making the short walk next door, Grace made sure that he had adequate supplies and that his arms were not paining him beyond the point of being able to look after himself. He thanked her quite sincerely for her help. That help, he discovered when he got indoors, had extended to asking Geordie's sister Hilda, who kept a key for emergencies, to go in and do the chores.

The bed was made and his breakfast dishes washed.

He took to his desk chair, leaned back and closed his eyes while his computer booted up. Then, his thoughts clarified, he got down to Delia Barrow's business. This, he had thought, would be like falling off a log but he soon found that it more resembled running through treacle. For a start, he had been out of the mainstream for two years and he had forgotten most of the data. His computer had crashed and been replaced, with considerable loss of addresses and phone numbers. On the phone but making much use of the Internet, he contrived to order a copy of Delia's birth certificate and a passport application form. During the intervals between 'I am putting you on hold' and 'If you want this service key that digit,' he had contrived to load and crop and print his photographs. He made much use of a small telephone amplifier to warn him when a real person was on the line.

It had been some time since the good but frugal hospital lunch. He poured himself a glass of wine and made a microwave snack that he took back to the computer. The telephone directory gave him several numbers for the Earl of Caithness. Office hours were past but he left a message on an answering machine to the effect that due to an unfortunate accident Mr Barrow would not be taking up the post. Delia had had no recollection of the wrecked car's registration number and was not even sure of the make and model, but at least she had remembered the name of the insurance company. He sent off an exploratory email, carefully worded to discover the policy number before revealing that neither his client nor her brother was able to quote it.

Evening was on him and the light outside was fading. Too late for contacting people in Britain, it was too early for business hours in New Zealand. He left his house by the front door, turned left and slipped through a gap in the hedge where Geordie had been in the habit of passing while he had had the care of the garden for Mr Sands.

Hilda answered the door and called her brother. Geordie was a small man of friendly if slightly clownish appearance. His head was as round as a ball and what little hair remained was dressed carefully across the top. In contrast to the immaculate little house, both he and his clothes were well worn; but the apparent anomaly was explained by the fact that he worked in the building industry and much of his time between contracts was given over to home improvement. He was accompanied to the door by a strong smell of paint. 'Mr Custer,' he said. 'I heard you were in hospital.' His voice had the soft lilt common to the Highlands but, as is normal in the far north, his use of the English language was excellent.

'I was,' Julian said. 'I'm just home.'

Geordie glanced down. The evening remained warm and Julian was still in shirtsleeves. 'Been quite the hero,' Geordie said. 'So I hear.'

'Not quite that,' Julian said. 'But I don't think I'm going to feel like moving my arms about much for some days and I seem to have taken on some desk-work. I was wondering if you could spare the time to do some decorating for me. Time-and-lime, of course.'

'Well, I don't know,' Geordie said slowly. 'I was wanting to give our whole downstairs a freshen up.'

Hilda had lingered to enjoy the social intercourse. She was a jolly, roly-poly person, always busy. 'Och,' she said. 'You can

44

fine spare the time, Geordie. There'll not be work for you at the Canmore House Hotel for weeks. That contract's had a setback.'

'You wouldn't have to start today,' said Julian. 'But I'm going to be busy and I want to be sure that somebody else will take it on. I've bought most of the paints.' He decided not to mention that one of the great hatreds of his life was preparing and painting skirting boards.

'If I'm to do it I'll do it now,' Geordie said. 'Give me tomorrow to gather my things and I'll start the day after.'

'That will be Saturday,' Hilda said. 'You're going to Inverness with Alec.'

'So I am, so I am. Monday, then.'

'Monday will suit me,' Julian said. 'In case I can't wait at home, try to come in and see me before that and I'll tell you what colour goes where.' As an afterthought, he asked, 'What went wrong at Canmore House Hotel? I was wondering why they were still closed with the season almost on them.' The proprietor, Derek McTaggart had been a friend years earlier and the hotel was just across the Firth from his house.

'The things people do!' Hilda said, indignant on behalf of the absent Derek. 'They were just ready to start replacing the old lead pipes as part of the contract for alterations, renovations and I-don't-know-what, when some men broke in at a weekend and stripped it all out.'

'I was supposed to be part of the gang that would be stripping it out,' Geordie said indignantly, 'and it was laid down, over and over, how we'd to be careful, only getting access where we were told to and opening up carefully, doing the least possible damage to the panelling and some bonny plaster cornices. But these buggers –' his sister drew in breath sharply at the word while at the same time nodding her agreement '– these buggers just ripped their way in, you'd hardly believe the damage they did. And all for the sake of some yards of lead piping. Losh, man, they could have earned twice as much honestly in the time, for all that they'll get for it; but some folk would rather have a crooked penny than an honest pound.'

Julian, from his early work as a defence solicitor, was able to agree. He returned to his house, which was simply called *Pog*. He had fallen for the house at first sight, despite the tasteless decor and the rigid garden, but

46

the name had nearly put him off until he discovered that the word was the Gaelic for *kiss*. None of the locals had been able or willing to tell him what romantic story had given rise to that choice of name. Somehow the presence of an obscure secret only added to the charm of the house.

A glance at his watch suggested that business hours should have begun in New Zealand. Delia had been sure that her share of the money from the sale of the family farm had been deposited with the South Island Bank in Christchurch. After a wrestle with Overseas Directory Enquiries he got a phone number. A further wrestle with a stubborn secretary was needed before he was introducing himself to the bank manager, but at last he began to make progress. The bank manager, Hopkins by name, had not known Delia personally, but within a few seconds – presumably using a computer – he had made himself aware of the very substantial sums in the accounts of Delia and her brother.

Julian explained briefly the accident and its consequences. 'You can see the bind that we're in,' he said. 'Miss Barrow has no identification with her except for her face, her signature, her voice, her passport when I manage to get her one and her recollection of PIN numbers and passwords. Unless you can suggest where her fingerprints or her DNA might be on record?'

There was a pause while Mr Hopkins thought. 'No,' he said at last. 'That I can't.'

'Well now. Your well-to-do client is caught without any cash, bank or credit cards or chequebook. And with one leg and one arm in casts, she is not fit to travel half round the world.'

'She's your client too,' Mr Hopkins pointed out.

'I know. And I have the same problem that you have. I'm not going to be her banker. So what steps do I have to take before you'll release her own money to her?'

'Let me think it over and I'll call you back. What's the number?'

Julian gave him the number. 'But bear in mind that it's evening here and I've been in hospital too. I'll be heading for bed soon.'

'I'll call you in the next hour or leave it until tomorrow.'

'That will do well.' Julian was feeling tiredness coming over him in waves, but the light snack of earlier in the evening seemed a distant memory. He prepared another and even lighter snack, designed to be easy on the digestion, and he was washing the few dishes when the phone rang. Mr Hopkins, good as his word, was on the line.

'Mr Custer? I've decided that we can't settle this at long range. This bank is associated with the Highlands and Islands Bank. They have an office in Inverness. I've just been looking at the map and that isn't far from you. I'm going to contact the manager there. We can work together but if you satisfy him you've satisfied me.'

'Let's try to satisfy everybody,' Julian said; but in his secret heart he knew that such an ideal is rarely achieved. He dragged himself up to bed and fell into an exhausted sleep.

Four

It seemed that the unusually warm spring weather had decided not to bother any more with the far north of Scotland. The morning was dry and calm. It was cool and cloudy but at least the sun, lower in the north of Scotland than in the rest of Britain, was not shining in a driver's eyes. Julian's arms were paining him. He was due to have the dressings renewed anyway, but in a sudden panic in case he was rubbing off the skin he telephoned the doctor's surgery. Both doctors were booked up until late afternoon, he was told, but if he came straight away...

He breakfasted on a glass of milk and a biscuit while he washed and shaved. He was in the car and out of the gate in record time and travelling clockwise around the Firth. The surgery occupied a new and modern building. The village was too small to support such a facility, but the surgery was strategically placed for buses and served several other villages and a surprisingly large agricultural hinterland.

Dr Sullivan, Julian had heard, was on the point of retiring – a point on which he had been perched for some years. Several retired doctors lived thereabouts and could be called in as *locum tenens* whenever one of the three regular doctors needed a holiday. Julian saw Dr Dawes, a dark and sallow young man who exuded the brisk confidence that most of us prefer to see in a doctor. Julian was relieved to find that Dawes was not one of the chatty types; he made a brief comment that he had heard about the fire, phrased in an obliquely congratulatory note. He then got on with dressing Julian's burns, which he pronounced to be mending satisfactorily and still free from infection.

With his forearms feeling much less as though they had been peeled with a blunt knife, Julian found himself back in the car. He could have returned home by the way he had come; but he was in no hurry to return to the effort and frustration of telephone, email and letter. The day was cooler, the sun less dazzling and the countryside was looking its best. It would not add so very much to his journey if he continued round the Firth in the clockwise direction and took a fresh look at the scene of the accident before returning home by way of the long, low bridge.

He parked where he had pulled up two days earlier. The wreck of the car had already been removed. The grass was still moist from the efforts of the firefighters. It was scorched black over a wide area but grass roots are not easily killed and he thought that much of it might regenerate. He quartered the ground but without expecting any discoveries. He was not disappointed. There was not a toffee paper nor a cigarette end to be found, but he had had to be sure. Delia Barrow's money and that of her brother, in the form of coins, would surely have survived the fire but when her purse or bag burned would have been deposited within the floor-pan of the car. It would probably not be worth reclaiming.

On the point of returning to his own car he saw that a smaller car in police livery had pulled in behind it. The uniformed officer who had arrived with the emergency services got out. In the confusion of the fire scene, with three emergency services struggling each to do the job and keep out of the others' way, he had been only one figure among many. Now Julian saw that he was young, thin and round featured. Julian, as a solicitor, had become used to finding policemen hostile and suspicious, but less formal attitudes often pertain in the Highlands and this one was neither. He made a friendly enquiry as to Delia Barrow's progress. Grace Campbell, he said, was a charming lady and her observations on the skid-marks in the road had put him in good odour with his superiors.

'I've been told to look into it,' he said, 'and see if there are any witnesses to be found. Other than yourselves, of course.'

The policeman's voice was the typical soft lilt of the region. Julian, although brought up not far away, had been sent away to school in Edinburgh. He could drop into the local tones if he wished but they did not come naturally to him. He decided not to make the effort. 'And are there any witnesses?' he asked.

'Not that I have found so far. Unless you count a farmer, Mr Donaldson of Craigieshaw, who was attending a sick beast beyond his hedge. He heard a vehicle go past and a minute later he saw the smoke above the trees. He is quite definite that he heard the sound of a diesel engine. The tracks in the road suggest a van rather than a car and, assuming that this was the same vehicle, the van was going slow and it was labouring up what is only a very slight hill. Make what you can of that.' He waited expectantly.

Julian could see where he was going and decided not to disappoint him. 'I'll tell you what I make of it. The van was overloaded, not speeding. When it turned into the main road, it understeered and crossed the road, forcing the oncoming car of the Barrows to run off the road. Is that how you see it?'

The policeman was nodding and smiling approvingly. Julian half expected a pat on the head. 'That is exactly how I see it,' said the PC. 'But why a vehicle should be coming out of there overloaded I do not yet understand. I will let you know if anything comes out of it. And you will let me know if the young lady recovers her memory?'

'Yes, of course. Tell me, where was the burnt car taken?'

Julian had no difficulty finding Mr Donaldson of Craigieshaw, but the farmer was unable to add anything to what he had told the traffic officer. Leaning back against his tractor's rear wheel, he would have been happy to discuss the weather, his beasts and the international situation indefinitely. Julian broke away without quite offending him. Returning towards the main road he decided that the incline would not stress an ordinary car but a heavily laden van would undoubtedly have to labour in low gear.

He set off for home, but when he was on the long bridge he decided to take a good look at the burnt car. The constable had told him that it had been removed to the police garage at Tain, where it was awaiting the instructions of Miss Barrow or her legal representative, and Tain was not far off his route. He headed past his turning for home and after a couple of miles turned off for Tain.

He had to produce the note of authorization that he had obtained from Dell before the mechanic at the police garage would allow him near her car although there would have been little for the most determined thief to steal. The mechanic levered the boot open for him but the luggage that had been inside had been over the ruptured petrol tank and was incinerated. Dell's handbag and her brother's briefcase had fared little better. The leather had turned to charcoal and the papers inside were powdered beyond recovery. He managed to recover a handful of coins from the floor pan, just as he had supposed. The remains of the vehicle would soon be incurring a storage charge. He bestowed the coins on the mechanic in exchange for a promise to dispose of the car when permitted. The days when a scrap car had a value to the seller were long gone.

He retraced his route as far as the roundabout and headed for home. A breeze had come up again and wavelets were dancing in the Firth.

He was black from his labours. A shower was necessary before he could settle at his desk with a large mug of coffee at his elbow. His first duty was to phone Delia Barrow. He got through to the ward and then to her bedside.

'Pretty bloody awful,' she said in answer to his polite enquiry. 'It's just catching up with me now, or else they're withdrawing the painkillers. Every bit of my body seems to be aching, not just the bone I broke, and I'm trying to develop the knack of remembering my brother without thinking about him more than a little. Does that sound quite mad?'

'It sounds very sensible. It may get you through this unhappy time. Your brother wouldn't have wanted you to suffer any more than you must.'

'Well, I dare say it'll be over in a year or two. Hey, and now the good news.' A smile came into her voice. 'My memory's coming back. I remember what ran poor Ally off the road. It was a van, either white or a very pale grey.'

'That agrees with what Mrs Campbell saw,' Julian told her. 'Was there any lettering on the sides?'

'Not a bloody thing that I remember. Just plain paint. I'd like to see that bastard hung out to dry for Ally's death and all the pain and trouble he's caused me, but I guess that that's kind of secondary. The important thing's to make me a real person again, with an identity and some money in the bank. They're not going to keep me in here for-ever.'

Julian began an explanation of what he was doing and what he intended to do to re-establish her identity, interspersed with detailed questions about her earlier life. 'I suggest that you start jotting down all these dates and your account and PIN numbers,' he said. 'Just in case your memory...' But it was evident that he was talking to himself. Sounds of surprise and pleasure were coming down the line. He thought at first that somebody had brought her food or delivered a kiss where it counted, but no.

'Oh no, it all seems quite clear now. I had a momentary flash of a pale coloured van coming at us out of a side-road on the right and Ally having to swerve to miss it. I guess he might have been better hitting it head-on, but then I might have been killed too.'

'Did you recall anything else?' Julian asked.

'Yep. This is what I wanted to say. The driver was a young guy. I don't remember what he looked like but he had a bandage round his head. There!'

'You're sure that it was a bandage and not a sweatband or something? It couldn't have been a short-haired woman with an Alice band?'

'It was a man with a bandage. I'm sure of it. I didn't have time to take in much about him, but my memory keeps insisting that he had a square sort of face and a blunt nose.'

'Well, that gives us a ten times better chance of catching up with him. But he was probably a joyrider in a stolen van.'

A pause on the line gave him time to drink his coffee.

'And maybe he was legit and with an insurance policy. Money wouldn't bring Ally back,' she said softly, 'but there's no point turning our backs on it. I might use it to set up a scholarship or something, in my brother's memory. Let's follow it up. I wish I could be more help but I'm kind of stuck here. I've been X-rayed and scanned and poked and prodded and they're sure there's no organic damage and my bone has started to knit well, but it'll still be a week yet before they'll trust me to the outside world. Maybe more.'

'Take your time. One, you'll do more damage if you try to walk too soon. And, two, it's going to take time to get you access to your bank accounts. For basic shopping, I can probably get you one or two credit cards – they seem to hand them out to everybody these days, down to the family cat; but you shouldn't use them for more than day to day expenditure. The accounts still have to be settled and they incur a steep rate of interest if they're not settled on time.'

'And when am I going to see you?'

'Soon enough. There will be things to sign and I'll probably have to bring somebody in to meet you and compare you with your photographs. For the moment, I want names and addresses of people who can swear to the subject of those photographs.'

'There's nobody in the UK except for some cousins in the Glasgow area who wouldn't be of any use – they haven't seen me since I was three.'

'Then we'll just have to depend on your friends and neighbours in New Zealand. Email addresses if you can remember them – that will be quicker.'

She made a face. 'None of them has ever seen me with make-up on and my hair tidy. It's very windy down there,' she said. 'If you do come here to visit, could you bring me some books?'

'Any particular authors?'

'I don't suppose you'd have any of my favourite New Zealand writers. Just any damn thing to help me pass the time. Not too damn heavy.'

In this technological age farming communities tend to rely heavily on email, but Delia had only been able to remember the email addresses of two correspondents who were also familiar with her appearance. Julian was composing his own email when he was interrupted by the phone.

'Mr Custer?' enquired a voice disbelievingly.

Julian suppressed a sigh. He had met the reaction before. It was the second-worst curse of having an unlikely name. (The worst was having to endure jokes about the Last Stand.) He agreed that he was indeed Julian Custer.

'My name is Fasque. I am the manager of the Inverness branch of the Highlands and Islands Bank. I have been contacted by the South Island Bank in New Zealand. I gather that your sister was recently killed in a car accident.' Mr Fasque's lilt was not quite the soft Highland lilt of the locality but inclined more to the slightly sibilant lisp of the west coast and the Hebrides.

'Not my sister,' Julian said quickly and firmly. 'My client. And Miss Barrow is not dead. I am acting as her solicitor.'

'Who then was killed?'

'Her brother. The cause of the crash is

under investigation.'

'I see.' There was a pause. It seemed that Mr Fasque was making notes. 'As I understand it, she lost all her documents in the subsequent fire. The young lady has a very substantial sum to her credit at the bank in New Zealand and her late brother had an even larger sum. I have been asked to make sure of the young lady's identity, after which her account could be transferred here or she could be afforded credit facilities if she decided to return to the Antipodes.'

'There would remain the matter of her brother's money,' Julian said. 'Unless a will turns up in New Zealand, I shall be asking a court to declare her his next of kin and therefore his heir.'

'She will be very comfortably situated,' said Mr Fasque.

'Yes indeed. I am attempting to obtain a replacement passport for her. That at least will make a first step towards proof of identity, because she is still a British citizen with a British passport so that her current photographs will resemble those deposited for the original passport application. The next step is for you to visit her in hospital with me and certify that the person in the photographs and supplying the sample signatures is the person claiming to be Delia Barrow. I can also send those to New Zealand where those who knew her will be able to certify before a JP that she is indeed Miss Barrow.'

Eventually, they agreed in principle on that course of action and disconnected. Julian blew out a long breath. Mr Fasque had proved to be a nit-picker. Although Julian himself was a lawyer, a profession which tends inevitably towards the picking of nits, he always tried to keep any discussion moving forward; but Mr Fasque had seemed to enjoy picking nits, not to advance the discussion and improve the final resolution but for the sake of the nits themselves, perhaps to add them to his collection. To such people, Julian knew, a neat page of figures or a well composed letter may be an end in itself and not a step along the road to a greater conclusion. But he also knew that there were ways of sticking pins into such people in a manner and location guaranteed to produce immediate action. The time for such drastic treatment, he thought, might not be far away.

Five

Freed for the moment from the fussiness of Mr Fasque, Julian returned to the preparation of an email to New Zealand. Well aware that out of any two email addresses one will certainly contain an error or be out of date or the addressee will have vanished into limbo, he prepared to send it to both the addresses remembered by Delia. If both responded, he would sort it out later.

After much thought and no little drafting and redrafting, he composed the following:

I have been given your address, by my client Miss Delia Barrrow, who I understand is a friend and former neighbour. Following an accident, Miss Barrow is at present in Raigmore Hospital, Inverness, where she is likely to remain for at least another week. Sadly, I must let you know that her brother, Aloysius, died in the same motor accident. In that accident and a subsequent fire, Miss Barrow also lost all her papers of identification. She has asked me to act as her solicitor. I write therefore to ask you:

Can you inform me of the name and address of Miss Barrow's solicitor in NZ?

If I were to email you copies of a good photograph of Miss Barrow, would you print or have printed, say, six copies and certify on the back of them, and on an accompanying sheet of paper in wording that I would give you, that they are a true likeness of Miss Barrow; and return them to me by air mail? If possible, your signatures should be executed before a JP and witnessed by a solicitor or by somebody of the status of a solicitor, an elected politician, an officer in the police or the armed services, or a clergyman.

Can you suggest the name etc. of anyone holding authentic examples of Miss Barrow's signature?

A prompt reply is desirable as Miss Barrow is unable to access her funds meantime.

Reading it over, he was inclined to delete mention of a politician; but then he reasoned that he would then have to delete mention of each of the other professions, except possibly the officers in the police or armed forces, as being no more dependable. He did, however, add *doctor* and *bank manager* to the list. He read it over again. There might be several other tasks necessary before Delia Barrow was once again established as a real and worthy member of the human race, but he preferred not to overload the recipient too soon. He closed with an expression of gratitude on behalf of Miss Barrow, signed it with his name and professional qualifications and sent it off.

With the identification of Miss Barrow pushed as far as he could see it go for the moment, he went next door to the right and knocked at Strathmore, the Campbells' house. Grace's car was by the door but there was no immediate sign of its owner. He was about to return home when Grace arrived on foot from the road. She was a picture bound to shock the more old-fashioned locals, wearing trainers, skimpy shorts and a T-shirt and she was sweating so that the two light garments clung to her, revealing every detail of a good and still youthful figure. Julian knew Grace for a fitness fanatic, as was suited to her profession. She had on occasions tried to persuade him to run, or at least to jog, along with her for company. Her husband regularly reminded her that the limp remaining from an earlier fall prevented him from moving at a pace faster than a walk. Julian, remembering that the man who invented jogging had died jogging, had so far resisted her invitations. Grace's massive golden retriever, Bonzo, had been loping along at her side but now broke away to meet Julian with a sniff, a snort, a head-butt and then a large paw.

'I'd like a word,' Julian said, releasing the big paw and turning his head in order to leave no doubt that he was requesting the word with Grace rather than Bonzo.

'Could it wait until this evening?' she asked. 'I have to go out to treat a patient.' She smiled wryly. 'An NHS patient, and they're the ones who scream loudest if they're kept waiting.'

'I don't think that this will take minutes.'

'Well, all right. But I must get out of these sweaty rags before I die of shame. Come and talk to me through the bathroom door while I shower.' She led him inside and along a brightly decorated passage.

Grace had travelled a lot and stayed in many easy-going households. This, combined with her medical background, had brought her to a state of unselfconsciousness about her body. Julian, on the other hand, was a member of a profession that knew only too well how an accidental glimpse could be turned into an episode of voyeurism. Moreover, he had been born with shyness towards women, which had been exacerbated by his earlier attempts at courtship. More recently, his professional life had kept him largely out of contact with the female of his species for several years. He sat where directed on a flimsy chair in Grace's bedroom, acutely and uncomfortably aware of the sounds of a lady disrobing at little (he tried not to think *barely*) more than arm's length.

'How's the girl doing?' she asked from the *en suite* bathroom. The damp T-shirt, shorts and a pair of minuscule pink pants landed on the floor near his feet. No bra, he could not help noticing.

'Very uncomfortable, but she seems to have started on the road to recovery. The big news is that her memory has begun to return. She bears you out to the tune of a white or pale grey van. A farmer heard it go by a few seconds earlier – overloaded rather than speeding. But the significant thing, and the reason that I wanted to catch you before you went out, is that the driver was a man who looked definitely young. She hardly had a glimpse of him but he had dark hair and a snub nose. One thing she's quite sure of is that he had a white bandage round his head.'

'Or a sweatband?'

'I asked her about that. She says not.'

While he spoke, Julian had been perturbed to notice that clean clothes and underwear had been laid neatly out on the bed beside him. There was also a large and fluffy bath towel. Her dressing gown hung behind the door. Was he expected to make himself scarce ... or to close his eyes ... or what?

Grace had to raise her voice to speak over the hiss of the shower. 'I see what you're after. I have the ear of the doctors and my husband is depute headmaster of the big school. Between us we should be able to find out which young man was wearing a bandage on Wednesday. Was that all?'

Julian realized that a mirror on the opposite wall gave him an oblique view into the bathroom where, made slightly hazy by steam, a figure of great charm was just rinsing off under the shower. 'That's the lot,' he said.

'And quite enough, too. Hang on. I'll be out in a minute.'

When Grace, wrapped in an enormous bath-sheet, emerged from the bathroom, Julian was not to be seen. From along the hall came the sound of the front door, closing.

Julian had a comfortable feeling that he had cast quite enough bread on the waters on behalf of his only client and could quite properly give some time to his own affairs and recreation until some of that bread floated home again, or until he had thought out what steps to take next.

But it was not to be. A travel-stained car, of medium size but bottom of the range, was parked crookedly on the gravel in front of his door and a man was hovering on the doorstep. The man's appearance was as undistinguished as his car. Nothing about him was noticeable – in fact, thinking about it later Julian realized that he could remember not a single detail of the man's face apart from the total lack of any departure from the humdrum norm. He was slightly stooped, his mousy hair was thinning and he had a slight pot belly. His suit, which had never been smart, was dusty and wrinkled and his shoes were in need of a good clean. In addition, the man gave an impression of being barely awake – an impression that Julian later concluded was carefully cultivated in order to trap the unwary into a sense of false confidence.

Looking somewhere over Julian's shoulder the man said, 'Mr Custer? May I have a word?'

'About what?'

The man hesitated and then said, 'About Miss Delia Barrow.'

'What about her?'

'I understand that she was involved in an accident.'

Julian felt his hackles rise. Had he been in a Shakespearean mood he might have suspected a pricking of his thumbs. The mention of Delia made him think of the telephone and he glanced at his sitting room window. The glass was reflecting the daylight but he knew precisely where to focus his eyes and he saw that the indicator light on his answering machine was flashing. If nothing else, a minute or two on the telephone might give him time to gather his wits. He certainly needed to update his information before discussing Delia with a representative of the press, however scruffy that representative might be.

'Wait here,' he said. He headed indoors and listened to the message. Delia had called and wanted him to call back. While he waited for the call to go through, he looked through the window. His visitor, unaware of being observed, was pacing around the garden but his attention was on the house and its surroundings and the contents of Julian's car. He was noticeably more alert. Julian had the impression that his eyes were not missing a detail.

Getting a connection to Raigmore Hospital took only a few seconds, but to speak to Delia entailed a long wait until the patients' telephone in her ward was free. By then, his visitor had seen enough and had retreated to lean against the wing of his car. Delia came on the line at last. 'There was a man here,' she said. 'He wanted to ask a whole lot of questions. But I made him tell me who he was first. He showed me a card so he may have been telling the truth. He's a reporter from Glasgow, name of Maclure. I asked him what paper he was from – his card didn't say – but he said that he was freelance.'

'What did you tell him?'

'Nothing. Not one damn thing. I thought I'd better speak to you first.'

'Well done,' Julian said. 'Tell me, what did he look like?'

His question seemed to take Delia aback. 'I really don't remember,' she said.

That, Julian realized, was an adequate description. 'He's here now. I'll find out what he's after. If you don't hear from me again on the subject, say nothing.'

'I can do that.'

'Your sex isn't usually very good at it,' Julian said warningly.

'I can be very good at it when I want.' He could hear the smile in her voice.

'Now would be a good time to show the world how good you are. If anybody asks you questions about the accident or about your inheritance – and this includes the police – refer them to me.'

They finished the call. Julian walked out but this time he was carrying a light, folding chair that lived in his hall. The man –

Maclure – moved forward as if expecting admission to the house but Julian opened the chair, set it down on the upper of the two steps and seated himself. 'Go ahead and ask your questions, Mr Maclure,' he said.

Maclure maintained an impassive expression; indeed, he might have been suppressing a yawn, but Julian was sure that a sharp brain was slicing through the available facts. Julian knew his name. He was not being admitted to the house. Julian's wrists were bandaged. Maclure decided on his approach. 'I believe that you're Miss Barrow's solicitor?'

'That's correct.'

'And that you witnessed the accident? That is a little unusual, isn't it?'

Julian had also decided on the line to be taken. To a lawyer, a carefully edited dosage of the truth is often the best medicine. 'I was not a witness. I arrived on the scene seconds after the crash. I was burnt while trying to rescue her brother so I travelled in to Raigmore in the same ambulance. That is how Miss Barrow came to ask me to act for her. She had lost her personal documentation in the fire and I am trying to help her to re-establish her identity.'

'And you were strangers until you met after the accident?'

'True.'

Mr Maclure yawned. 'I understand that there's a large sum of money in dispute?'

So, Julian thought, this was not the sort of question to be expected from a journalist who was merely reporting on a fatal accident. 'Miss Barrow's brother leaves a substantial sum,' he said. 'I am not aware that there is any dispute. As her solicitor I would expect to be the first to know.'

Mr Maclure's manner became even more casual. 'Isn't it rather unusual for a witness to an accident to act for one of the parties?'

'It would be,' Julian said. 'But the accident had already happened before I came on the scene. I only witnessed the sudden ignition of the spilled fuel. I was not a witness to the accident nor are there any other parties involved.'

'So far.'

'So far,' Julian agreed. 'Are you telling me that there may be other parties?'

Mr Maclure allowed his lackadaisical air to slip. 'I didn't come here to tell you anything,' he said. 'I came to ask one or two questions.

If you don't want to answer them—'

'You'll conclude that I have something to hide.'

'Do you?'

'There we go! No, Mr Maclure, I do not have anything to hide. But nor do I have any obligation to tell you any more than you tell me. In fact, I have just as much right to ask questions as you have. Who has been feeding you duff information and just what did they suggest?'

Mr Maclure moved uneasily from foot to foot. Being obliged to stand while Julian sat seemed to be irking him. 'My sources are privileged and confidential.'

'Editors have ended in jail for trying that argument,' Julian said.

'In court, yes. Outside it, I don't have to reveal my sources. As to what they suggested, you can read about it. Had you ever met Miss Barrow prior to her accident?'

'No. I had not,' Julian stated flatly. 'In fact, she had only been in Britain for a couple of days and was passing through this area for the first time. I haven't been abroad for years. I have never been to New Zealand in my life.'

'Is Miss Barrow her brother's only beneficiary?'

'No comment, but only because I have not yet seen his will. Now please go. Or do I have to eject you forcibly?'

'You think you could?'

'I'm damn sure I could.'

Maclure looked fully awake and belligerent. Julian had not been a man of violence but he had acquired some knowledge of self-defence. Maclure might look feeble but his background suggested that he might be a dirty fighter. Without moving, Julian made mental preparations to rise quickly and use his chair as a weapon. But Geordie Munro chose that moment to come through the gap in the hedge.

Maclure recognized that he was outnumbered. He invested a nod with ominous significance, returned to his car and drove off. With Geordie's arrival, Julian brought his mind back to the matter of his house and its décor. He led Geordie to the room that was destined to become the study. It was a well-proportioned room with a good window overlooking the ever-changing view of the Firth, but it had been painted an uncompromising, institutional green even to the ceiling. 'Do this room first,' Julian said. 'And quickly. I think I'll go mad if I have to live with this colour for long.'

Between men, it took very few words to convey the desired colour scheme. Julian placed a large can of paint on the table that had been serving him as a desk, pointed at the ceiling and said, 'White'. Two smaller cans followed. He pointed to the skirtings, the window and the door surrounds and said, 'Grey'. The biggest can, holding a pale but warm blue-grey, only merited the word 'This' and a sweep of the hands around the walls.

'Right,' Geordie said. Eight words had sufficed to establish an agreement that each would honour.

That settled and Geordie departed, Julian felt free to change into his oldest clothes. With the whole interior of the house to be decorated he would continue to live out of his suitcases for a while, only airing and ironing whatever would be needed next, but at least he could get into the garden. In anticipation, he had purchased, at great expense, a range of the best gardening tools in stainless steel and these were waiting in the darkness of a garden shed near the bottom of the lawn.

It had been some time since he had had the pleasure of working in a garden that he could call his own. Among his purchases had been an electric lawnmower that he would have enjoyed taking for a test run, but Geordie had been engaged by the previous owners of *Pog* to keep the garden tidy and Julian had been happy to have him continue with the mowing. So Julian began to tackle the weeds that had seeded themselves in the borders. He began to dig, pausing only to toss the bigger weeds on to the grass where they could wither and die or be chopped up by the next pass of the mower. It was soon time to straighten his back and look around. He went back to work slightly dispirited. Even when all was weed-free and saved from the slight shagginess of neglect it would not be a beautiful garden, just a rectangle of ground divided into smaller rectangles by straight paths that went nowhere in particular. Geordie had been engaged to keep the garden and this he had done according to his lights by scattering the seeds of the gaudier annuals or reserving some beds for vegetables. It had all the *joie de vivre* of the worst kind of municipal graveyard, the sort in which, Julian decided, he would come back from the dead rather than accept burial. It needed to be redesigned but he had not the faintest idea how to set about it. He had a vague mental picture of the right sort of garden but when he tried to focus on it the details dissolved and the form refused to accommodate itself to the boundaries of *Pog*'s garden.

A well-grown hedge divided the garden of *Pog* from that of the Campbells next door, but Julian peered through a slight gap. He had only previously seen the Campbells' front garden, which was mostly of inter-locking brick car space with some grass, a hedge and a pair of trees. But the sweep of garden behind the house, he now saw, was a natural-looking and exceptionally beautiful mini-landscape. It had that look of having just plain happened which he knew to be the result of a great deal of contriving. Among the apparently random spreads of shrub and ground cover were splashes of colour which just happened (or so it seemed) to harmon-ize to perfection. A little study suggested that there was plenty of colour to come later in the year and foliage or bright stems for winter colour. If this had been Grace's in-spiration, a little brain-picking was definitely called for.

He had his chance late that afternoon. He had knocked off for what he considered to be a well-earned drink, which would have been followed by a shower and a meal, with a check on his emails fitted in somewhere in between. When Grace arrived, he was hesitating between whisky with a beer chaser as against rather good supermarket boxed claret. She made his decision for him by joining him in his sitting room and accepting a glass of the claret. Julian was pleased by the arrival of an attractive woman to decorate his room. The solitary life was beginning to pall. He would have to look around for a replacement girlfriend and make a real effort to conquer the reserve that had rendered his adult life so monastic.

Grace's visit was for no more purpose than to report that she had spread her enquiries abroad. She had been unable to make contact with any of the local nurses, but she had left messages begging them to advise her if any of them had bandaged a young manhead within the past week or so.

Julian thanked her politely but his mind had moved on from Delia Barrow's problems for the moment. 'Are you the gardener of the family?' he asked.

She looked at him in surprise. 'Lord no!' she said. 'Why?'

'Your garden looks so natural and so beautiful. Your husband's work, perhaps?'

Grace chuckled at the very idea that Stuart would be a boon to any garden. 'He's worse than I am. The green on his fingers is arsenical weedkiller. The person you want is May Largs. She was brought up in Dornoch but she lives in Beauly now. It's almost a fifty-mile run each way but she still has a lot of clients and an elderly mother here so she comes through quite often. She works with two of the horticultural firms. You pay for what you get, and what you get doesn't exactly come cheap, but what you do get is the sort of garden you're talking about – one that's designed to look like a piece of nature while giving you well arranged colour for most of the year. And one that's very easily kept, which saves the cost of getting somebody in.'

'That's exactly what I want,' Julian said.

'Then you're in luck. She's become a friend of mine. Would you like me to phone and find out when she'll be through this way? I know you don't like being helped.'

He had to smile. 'Was I really so ungracious? Put it down to a fierce determination to stand on my own feet and you can blame my bossy mother. In this instance, I'll be very grateful.'

'Just in case you say anything out of place or need some special kind of help, I'd better tell you that her husband is a very senior detective. He doesn't do any favours in business, but he can sometimes help with advice.'

Julian reached for a pencil. 'Mrs Largs, did you say?'

Six

He had expected to be left in peace and boredom for the weekend – perhaps brooding over Dell, who seemed to be monopolizing his thoughts – while the recipients of his emails digested his messages and while many offices were closed. But it seemed that others had also been busy. His morning mail brought a passport application form; and an envelope from the insurance company containing a claim form and duplicate policy documents. He put the forms aside to complete at his leisure and opened his email.

Here, also, his correspondents had been busy. An email from New Zealand read:

Miss Anderson has passed to me your email, as a JP and as the minister of the church attended by the Barrow family, regarding the death of Aloysius Barrow. The community sends heartfelt sympathy to Delia.

If you will forward the photographs to me as you suggest, I will see that they are properly attested.

I understand that Aloysius and his sister both used the firm of Hudson and Larks, attorneys.

It was signed, *Gilbert Franklin, DD, JP.* with a postal address attached.

The man of God, being also a JP and therefore more businesslike than many of his colleagues, also appended the address in Christchurch, the phone number and the email address of the lawyers. The Barrow

84

family must have been popular in their neighbourhood. There followed six emails expressing sympathy, for relaying to Delia. Three of them also sent money orders to be used for flowers whenever the funeral of Aloysius took place.

In all honesty, Julian would have had to admit that after a day during which he had made much use of muscles that had become unaccustomed to such labour as digging, he was not keen to resume hard physical graft. He settled down quite cheerfully to composing a suitable email to Mr Franklin, asking him to thank the well wishers on Delia's behalf and suggesting a suitable form of words for endorsing the photographs. He attached the best three photographs from among those that he had taken in the hospital, inviting Mr Franklin to select the one most typical of Miss Barrow, and he concluded by suggesting, without quite promising, that any expenses would be reimbursed.

Another email to Hudson and Larks advised them of the death of Aloysius Barrow and enquired whether they were holding his will or any other crucial documents. If so, would they please tell him the identity of the executor. He attached a photograph of Delia and a fax of her holograph letter of appointment and he signed it with his full name and qualifications.

A glance at the insurance claim form suggested that another word was due with Grace Campbell, as an almost witness to the accident, but it was Grace's habit to go for a run whenever she was not committed to a patient in the morning. He had no wish to be urged to join in any such exercise nor to be in the vicinity of the succeeding shower. He waited until he saw her return and then gave it a further quarter-hour before picking up his camera and venturing next door. Grace – neat, fresh and respectable as almost always – admitted him and they sat down to coffee in her sitting room. He had glimpsed Stuart, Grace's husband, relaxed in a deckchair on the lawn.

'I've just sent off the photographs of Delia to New Zealand,' he said. 'For the first time, I scrolled back to photographs taken earlier. You seem to have taken some shots around the wreck and the fire.'

Grace shrugged and forced another biscuit on him. 'The policeman took the shots of the roadway and he showed me how to use your camera. It seemed silly to be standing there with a camera in my hand, one that doesn't cost anything for film, and not to make a record while I waited for somebody to take my statement and finish with me.'

Julian agreed. He asked a few questions to clarify the subjects and angles for purposes of the insurance claim. 'Would you write me out a statement about the whole incident as you saw it?'

'I'll do it tomorrow. If that's all for the moment,' Grace said, 'I can tell you that I was going to speak to you. I have some news. May Largs – the horticultural designer – phoned me. She was coming this afternoon to have a look at the garden at Cannaluke Lodge, the other side of the Firth. That's one of her biggest and best projects; it figures in gardening books and tourist guides and I don't know what. Some fresh photographs are needed, now that some of the planting has matured, and she wants to be sure that it's all neat and tidy. I've asked her to lunch. Will you join us? No need to dress up.'

'Love to,' he said.

He filled in the rest of the morning selecting and printing photographs to accompany the claim form. When an unfamiliar car rolled up next door, he checked himself in the mirror for tidiness and then walked round by the road.

May Largs, he discovered, was a small, dark-haired, rather shy woman tending towards a not unattractive plumpness. Stuart, Grace's husband, was a good-looking man entering middle age, with a small beard and a limp that became noticeable when he was tired. He had vanished but soon reappeared having readied himself for guests.

The first order of business was a guided tour of the garden, accompanied and supervised by the ever-present Bonzo. A curtain of thin cloud hid the sun but there was no hiding the beauty of the garden. The satisfaction expressed by both the Campbells was evidently genuine and justified. May was quite prepared to explain her reasoning for every shape and choice of planting. Each was obviously right and in the right place, yet the result of careful consideration. The outcome was charming, natural and harmonious and, because no gaps between the ground cover were left for weeds, would require the minimum of maintenance. Every single plant seemed to be thriving, which was unique in Julian's experience.

The cost of the design and execution, revealed frankly although in round terms, had not been small; but for his own garden, which was of similar size, the cost would be manageable out of his recently settled fees and, as an alternative to endless labour arriving at the end in an amateurish result, began to look like a sound economy and a source of pleasure for years to come. In the past, he had often noticed that a wild but considered extravagance, once made, became history. The first cost was soon forgotten but the pleasure was more lasting. He promised to think about it, but with an unspoken decision to go ahead unless some insuperable objection should occur to him during the cooling-off period that he usually allowed himself before some major commitment.

It was over lunch that he was granted an additional boon. The meal was taken in a smart new dining room. This had been created in what had once been a spare bedroom; previously, meals had been taken in the kitchen. The meal was vegetarian to avoid offending against one of Julian's prejudices and because May was perpetually fighting weight-gain, but Grace had contrived a very tasty moussaka. May, after eyeing Julian's bandages, made a polite enquiry and so had to be regaled with an account of the car smash, the fire and the predicament of the luggage-less and temporarily penniless Delia.

'Well, it sounds to me as though you were very brave,' May said. 'And did nobody set eyes on the other vehicle?'

'Miss Barrow remembers a white or pale grey van. One might suspect that memory was playing her false due to the heat of the moment – my car was once hit by a post office van but I was left convinced that it had been a Rolls Royce. However, Grace saw a white or pale grey van leaving the scene, so they may both have been blessed with twenty-twenty visual memory on this occasion, in which case the driver was a young man with a bandage on his head.'

'I could point you to about a hundred white or pale grey vans,' said May. 'But about your young man with a bandage on his head. I may be able to help. Of course, there may have been a dozen young men going around with bandaged bonces around that time.'

'Then we may have to eliminate them one at a time,' Grace said. 'Go on, May.'

May took a few seconds to clean the last

mouthful from her plate. 'It must have been last Tuesday,' she said. 'I was at the Brierly Hotel garden, where Horticom is doing some work for me. Actually, I'd done everything short of planting the tubers myself but they'd still managed to confuse the colours. Anyway, one of the youngsters was using a power tool, I forget just what, and the silly ass had left the key in the chuck. As soon as he pulled the trigger the key flew like a bullet and hit another boy, who was yards away, right on the brow. They were both lucky that it missed his eye.

'There was blood all over the place and a punch-up threatening, but luckily the boss, Mr Hodges, was on site and he soon sorted them out. He sent the offender home with a flea in his ear and took young Dean in his own car to get a deep cut stitched and bandaged. When he came back, Mr Hodges said that they hadn't used sutures for the sake of the scarring and instead they'd sort of glued it up and bandaged him. Dean had wanted to come back to work but Mr Hodges said that he wasn't taking any chances on one of his men working with concussion or a hairline skull fracture. Mr Hodges is a model employer. Also, I think he was envisaging Dean collapsing with an intracranial haemorrhage and suing the pants off him. He'd sent Dean home for the rest of the week and read him a list of symptoms that he was to dash straight to the doctor if he experienced any of, if you can understand me.'

'We understand you, even if you are a bit garbled,' said Stuart, the depute headmaster. 'But Dean who?'

'Dean Murray. You must remember him?'

Julian, glancing around, saw amusement reflected in each face and wondered what could be coming.

'I do indeed,' Stuart said. 'Clever young devil, but wild. He had quite a talent for drawing. I hoped that he was going to do something with it.'

'I remember him with affection,' said Grace, 'and I never even met him. One kept hearing stories about his jokes. You remember the time he was driving his father's Land Rover on the single-track roads and some other farmer's tractor driver, with a load of straw bales on a trailer, could easily have pulled into a passing-place and let him by but gave him two fingers instead?'

The others nodded but Julian said, 'No.

Remember, I'm a comparative newcomer. Tell me.'

'Well, Dean got out and ran after the tractor,' she explained to Julian, 'and cut the binder twine that was holding the bales together. A whole mountain of straw poured off into the road but Dean turned in the width of the road and went round the other way. It might have ended there except that a police car came along while the tractor driver was trying to pick up his straw and they made a case of it.'

'The sheriff almost said aloud that he'd often felt like doing the same thing,' said Stuart. 'He fined Dean the absolute minimum and then awarded the farmer about a fiver in damages. Young devil!' he added. Julian assumed that he was referring to young Dean rather than to the tractor-driver, the farmer or the sheriff.

'But he is doing something with his drawing,' May said. 'He'll never be an artist but his drawings are brilliant. He's only working for the landscaping contractor while he tries to get established as a cartoonist, but they find him useful, illustrating some of my designs and their own. He's had several cartoons published. The one I remember best was published in the *Sunday Sun* at the time that the local authorities were trying to clean up the graffiti. It showed a brick wall with a big white splodge on it. Stencilled in the splodge was the shape of a man who was in the act of writing on the wall. The writing said, "Keep graffiti away, spray a vandal today." Well, I thought it was quite witty. I believe he was quite well paid for it.'

'He didn't get paid for the stunt he pulled on the radio station,' said Grace.

'What stunt was that?' Julian asked.

'We didn't hear it ourselves,' Grace said, 'because we don't listen to pop, but there's some disc jockey on a live request show who always asks the younger callers, especially girls, in a very patronizing voice, where they're sitting before playing their choice of record. It may only be meant as an easy way to break the ice and to get them talking, but it must have been asking for trouble, especially on a live show, and Dean was just the lad to provide it. He got a girl to phone up and when she was asked where she was sitting she said, "On the toilet," and Dean blew an enormous raspberry. There was quite a row about it but they never made a case. Too difficult to prove, they said, but I suspect that the reason was more that it wasn't the sort of case that a fiscal wants to argue in front of a jury. I'm afraid that's the sort of way Dean's sense of humour works, which may put a limit to his career as a cartoonist.'

'Not in this day and age,' Stuart said.

It was clear to Julian that the others thoroughly disapproved of young Dean but enjoyed his humour. Julian would rather have liked to hear some more samples of it, but no doubt opportunities would follow.

'Where does he live, this Dean Murray?' he asked.

'His father has a small farm near Inveran,' May said. 'Dean's usually resident there, but he has a lot of friends, not all of them exactly reputable, and he bunks down with one or another of them quite often.'

Julian treated these revelations to a few seconds of rapid thought. 'I mustn't go off half-cocked,' he said. 'On the other hand, Miss Barrow's insurers may look on her with a jaundiced eye if she makes a claim in respect of a car insured by her brother and written off two days later. They may be more inclined to settle if we can name another driver who ran her brother off the road. How can I find out whether he has the use of a white or pale grey van?'

'On your own, he'll probably give you the runaround,' Grace said. 'I could come with you this afternoon, if you like. I'm known locally.'

'That would be perfect,' Julian said. Out of the corner of his eye he saw that Stuart was looking less than happy. 'If Stuart doesn't mind,' he added.

'As long as it doesn't make us too late at dinner,' Stuart said. 'It's not that I don't trust the pair of you. I just hate going to bed on a full stomach. And I'm a rotten cook.'

'He's a very good cook really,' Grace said. 'He just won't admit it in case he ends up doing his fair share. But it's all prepared,' she told her husband, 'and if you turn the oven on at about four o'clock all will be well. About one-eighty and you know which oven. I'll be back in time to deal with the vege-tables.'

Seven

They left as soon as May Largs had taken the hint and made her departure. They took Julian's car. His forearms had become less sensitive to the rub of his dressings, so he drove. He set off at no great pace. 'There's no hurry,' he said. 'If Stuart turns your oven on at four, you won't be needed until about five, probably five-thirty, so we have time in hand. Right?'

'True as far as it goes,' Grace said. 'But you may have forgotten, if you ever knew it, that there's no such thing as a short visit up here, except among incomers who don't know any better. This is a country area and until recently there was no entertainment except gossip. Custom requires that the visitor be given a cup of tea and probably a dram and that news be exchanged about every common acquaintance.'

'Surely you exaggerate?' Julian said. Much

of his youth had been spent in boarding schools. Of the remainder, he remembered being dragged on visits that had seemed interminable, but he had usually been allowed to go outside to wander or play with a companion and he had assumed that his parents were transacting some sort of family business indoors.

'Perhaps,' Grace said. 'But not very much. You'll see.'

Julian picked up speed, as much as the narrow and twisting roads would allow. Guided by Grace, he headed round the western end of the Firth by Bonar Bridge and soon left the secondary roads behind for single-track roads with passing places. The ancient hills, smoothed by time, were based on solid rock with huge outcrops escaping above the surface. The heather had not yet flushed its remarkable pink. Julian slowed once for a family of grouse picking grit beside the road. Here and there overflowing rivers and streams had left deposits of sedimentary soil so that, among land that was devoted almost entirely to forestry or sheep and grouse, unexpected little arable farms produced oats or potatoes or reared semi-free-range poultry.

The Murray farm, Diebreach, straddled Breach Water, an insignificant stream that twisted and turned along the bottom of a valley once ploughed by a glacier between hillsides that glowed with clumps of gorse in full yellow flower. The road found it more convenient to follow a straighter and more level path along the side of a minor mountain. Grace stopped Julian just short of a crest and they walked forward a few yards. Diebreach came into view – a few fields showing different shades of green, a double-fronted house, presumably of stone but now roughcast, with dormer windows in the slated roof. A single bored-looking cow dominated a small paddock. Several sheds of varying sizes and a collie sheepdog lying patiently in the shade of a tractor completed the scene. In the lee of the house was a Land Rover. The tractor and the Land Rover each seemed to be of long outdated designs.

'No sign of young Dean,' Julian said. 'Or of a white van.'

'Nor of anybody else.'

'Maybe they're out. It's Saturday.'

'There's smoke at the chimney. What do you want to do?'

Julian's thinking had not progressed so far

ahead. He pondered hurriedly. 'All I want is a word with him. Or, even better, a chance to ask others where he was last Wednesday and whether he had the use of a pale van. At the risk of warning him that he's on my speak-to list, let's just go down and ask. You can do the talking.'

'And just what am I supposed to say?'

'Let's be quite open and above-board until we have reason to stop. Say that we're looking for witnesses to an accident.'

'That's a real lawyer's remark,' Grace said. ' "Quite honest until we have reason to stop".' She was still chuckling as Julian nursed his car carefully down a steep farm road where successive storms had washed away much of the surface leaving the tops of underlying boulders exposed. Julian was forced to pick his way with great care rather than risk knocking off his silencer. As they pulled up beside the tractor, under the unblinking gaze of the collie, a middle-aged man emerged from the house. He was of slight build but he looked muscular. His expression was friendly.

'Good afternoon,' Grace said. 'I'm Grace Campbell.'

'Aye. You'll be the physio lady. You attended to my Aunt Jessie.'

It was an introduction but an appropriate reply was also necessary. Grace did a mental scan for Jessies among her past clientele. 'That would be Jessie McNaught. How is her arthritis now? Does it still pain her?'

'Not in thc lcast. Shc dicd in January.' This was said not as a joke but as a factual reply to a simple question. 'Come away in.'

They were led into a dark sitting room, furnished comfortably but in old-fashioned style with a worn three-piece suite finished in dark moquette. The grate was empty – evidently this room was not heated unless visitors were expected. Mr Murray called to 'Mother' to put the kettle on for visitors.

When they were seated, Grace said, 'This is Julian Custer. You may have heard about the car that crashed and burnt near Clashmore during the week?' (Mr Murray nodded.) 'Mr Custer was burnt, trying to save the young man that died.' Julian noticed that her Highland lilt, which was barely noticeable in her customary speech, had become stronger.

'That was well done,' said Mr Murray respectfully, glancing at Julian's bandages.

'Not so well,' said Julian. 'He died anyway.

In fact, I believe he was dead before I got near him.'

'But one must try,' said the farmer. 'Just as long as there is the least wee bit of hope, one must try.' His manner suggested that Julian had gained full marks for courage and for modesty.

'I was following close behind,' Grace said. 'Julian's my next-door neighbour, he bought *Pog,* where Andrew and Jenny Sands used to live when they were in Britain, and we were taking my car for its MOT. There were signs on the road that another car might have been involved, if only by making the driver swerve, so we're looking for witnesses. For the insurance, you understand. Mr Custer is a good friend of the sister of the man who died. We were hoping to have a word with your Dean. Is he at home?'

'No, he is not.' The farmer sat himself up very straight. 'What has our Dean to do with this?'

'Nothing, as far as we know,' she said. The farmer began to relax. 'But a young man with a bandage on his head was seen in that area and we wondered if Dean had seen anything.'

'No. He would have said.'

'You have seen him since then?'

'No. We have spoken on the phone.'

Grace looked mildly surprised. 'Surely he would not be likely to mention having seen a motor accident? Where was he speaking from?'

'That I do not know,' said Mr Murray. 'He telephoned to say that he might not be home for a few days. He had been in a small accident himself at his work and his employer had told him to take the rest of the week off, in case of a concussion.'

Grace was uncertain what to ask next and Julian hesitated to push the questioning to the point at which the farmer's defensive hackles might be raised again, so each was relieved at the entry of Mrs Murray, carrying a tray and explaining that the kettle had already been near the boil. Tea and scones were distributed, introductions made and explanations repeated for the visit and for Julian's bandages.

Mrs Murray was duly admiring of Julian's courage and sense of duty, but further discussion was delayed by the need to explore the local connections of both Julian and the Barrow siblings. Even these digressions were subject to further digressions until Julian was quite sure that the farmer was doing his utmost to hold the conversation away from the subject of his son. This serial evasion Julian found amusing, but eventually he was driven to say, 'Then you can't suggest where Dean might be?'

'We have no way of knowing that,' said the farmer, but his wife, ignoring warning signals from her husband, said, 'Och now, Dad, you know that he most often stays with Fergus Donelly.' It took only a little more coaxing to obtain Fergus Donelly's address.

As they were preparing to leave, Julian directed a meaning glance at Grace. Grace said, 'Would Dean ever have the use of a van, white or pale grey?'

Mr Murray was showing signs of unease after his wife's frankness. Before she could reveal any more he said quickly, 'Och, everybody has access to one of those, They're the commonest colours of vans to be hired.'

'I suppose that's true,' Julian said. He wrote his phone number on a page of his little notebook and tore it out. 'When Dean comes home, please ask him to call me at this number. It really is important. Tell me, how is he getting on at his work?'

'He is doing fine at the landscaping,' said

the farmer. His face clouded. 'We hope that he will stick to it. There is a future there. He is clever with his pencil, there is not the least doubt about that, but is there a living to be made at it I wonder?'

'There are some who make a very good living at it,' Julian said. 'But the best of the living goes to the very few of the very best.' As he spoke, he found that his own speech was returning towards the lilt of his youth.

'From what he tells me,' said the farmer, 'his drawing is useful when he illustrates designs for gardens that the firm is quoting for. That is a proper use for the knack, not doing rubbishy jokes for the daily papers.'

The Murrays both came out to the car with them. As Julian prepared to drive off, Mrs Murray said, 'If you hear anything, please let us know.' She said it quickly before her husband could cut her off.

'Of course I will,' Julian said.

As he guided the car cautiously up the rutted track, he said, 'What did you make of that?'

Grace took a few seconds before replying. 'I think that they're both anxious. He's fond of his son but the boy's a skellum. He's talented and he's funny but he's easily led into mischief. His father doesn't want to make waves in case his son's in trouble. Judging from the way his expression changed, I think that what Mr Murray knows about Fergus Donelly may not be the kind of things that a father finds reassuring.'

'Do you know anything about this Fergus Donelly?'

'Not a thing. I suggest that you make enquiries before doing any more in that direction. Your pal in Traffic might be your best avenue.'

Julian managed not to point out that he had already thought of that expedient for himself, but it took an effort.

'I think we should head for home now,' Grace said. 'I'd like to check that Stuart has started the meal cooking. If he's got his head in a book or found something gripping on the Internet, anything could be forgotten. I would ask you in, only – '

'Don't even think of it,' Julian said. 'I have something out of the freezer and half thawed already.'

Julian made preparations for his own evening meal but it was too early for cooking to begin. He picked up the phone and keyed the number for the local police, intending no more than to set up an appointment with PC Weigh. As it turned out, however, PC Weigh was doing his turn at weekend duty on patrol and was in the vicinity of Evelix, not far away. His blue and white panda car arrived at the door a few minutes later.

'I'm free for the moment,' he said, 'on the understanding that I may be called away at any time.'

'Understood,' Julian said. 'When does your shift finish?'

'At six.'

Julian nodded. He recounted what he had learned from Delia, May and the Munros. He was interrupted once when the personal radio attached to PC Weigh's collar began to quack out a message, but the information about the recovery of a stolen car in Dingwall required no immediate action.

The constable listened intently to what Julian had to tell him. Unlike some of his colleagues further south, he had no objection to discussing a case with a member of the public. 'There would seem to be a possibility – only a possibility,' he said cautiously, '– that young Dean Murray was driving the light coloured van. The van was overloaded, that much has been confirmed by forensic study of your photographs. That opens up another possibility. You heard about the theft of lead piping from the Canmore House Hotel? One of those selfish crimes.'

'I would have considered all crimes to be selfish,' Julian said, trying not to smile at the other's indignation.

'Not at all,' said PC Weigh reprovingly. 'If somebody picks your pocket, he gets your money but you only lose just the same amount. That is wrong but it is understandable. These thieves did far more damage than stealing the pipes. They ripped them out, damaging much of the finish of the place, and then left the water pouring out. The value of the lead was not so great, if fact I am surprised that they did so much work for so little reward, but perhaps they did not realize the labour that they were setting themselves. The cost of the damage and the replacement of the pipes is many times more than the value of the lead. And, of course, there is the lost business. The hotel will not reopen until the season is half gone. I can understand even if I do not approve of somebody taking something that he wants; but to take something that will cost the owner many times more than you will get for it, that I consider selfish.'

Julian nodded. He had felt much the same when required by the legal aid system to defend an addict who had mugged an old lady. Even so, it seemed to be a very Highland way of looking at it.

PC Weigh resumed. 'But I was saying. We have no evidence of a link, but is it stretching coincidence to suppose the theft of lead and an overloaded van, in this quiet corner of the Highlands, is not to be connected? I shall make a report. You have not gone near this Fergus Donelly?'

'I thought it better to speak to you first,' said Julian.

'Very wise. His reputation is not of the best. I am not surprised that Mr Murray, who is a respectable farmer and well thought of hereabouts, showed concern. I have no doubt that the name of Fergus Donelly is being considered in connection with the theft, but we must now start considering him in connection with the fatal accident. You represent the sister of the deceased, so I will be obliged to keep you informed.' He paused and a solemn look sat unnaturally on his usually bland and contented face. 'But there is much that they are not telling me. They ask me questions and then go into a huddle from which I am excluded. But I will tell you what I can when I learn it.'

'I'll be grateful,' Julian said. 'And now I see that it's past six o'clock and your shift is finished. Would you care for a drink?'

PC Weigh's face lit up. It was the first time that Julian had seen him smile. He settled back comfortably into his chair. 'I'm in sore need of a dram. But just the one. I still have to return the panda car to Dornoch.'

Julian was on the point of heading for bed when his telephone summoned him into the study. The call, over a very clear line, was from New Zealand. Mr Hopkins, the bank manager, identified himself. 'You're not recording this?' he asked.

Julian said that he was not.

'Keep it that way. The police have been asked to ask questions on behalf of your police in Scotland. They've been on to the lawyers and Mr Hudson spoke to me. He's been told to keep it under his hat but nobody told me anything like that so I'm passing the word along. Miss Barrow is well thought of around here. One of my daughters was at school with her.'

'Go on,' Julian said.

'Our Christchurch police have been using the heavy weapons. They got a judge to side with them, granting court orders. They wanted to know how much is in the bank accounts and how the money's left.'

'It would soon become a matter of open record. I can't claim that I'm very surprised. Somebody has been making enquiries and spreading muck. If you told the police, you'd better tell me.'

'I guess so.' The banker quoted figures. Julian had already realized that substantial sums must have been deposited. He had just been dealing with the shipping arbitration and his carefully calculated awards had been in respect of sums that he would normally have considered staggering. Otherwise he would have felt overwhelmed by the value of a large and well-stocked sheep station. Even so, his eyebrows went up when the figures were quoted. If all or most of her brother's money had been left to Delia, he could quite see that to a Highland policeman such a legacy would be like winning the national lottery.

'Do you happen to know how the money is

left?' he asked.

'I understand from Mr Hudson that each made a will naming the other as beneficiary.'

He thanked the banker and rang off.

Instead of going to bed he settled in the kitchen with a large whisky and a bowl of breakfast cereal. The police, it seemed, could find motivation for all sorts of misdeeds and somebody was taking pains to stir up their suspicions. When he came to recall Delia Barrow he found it impossible to give credence to any of them. He went to bed in the end but sleep was slow to come.

Eight

Julian again expected a lazy day. Sunday was never a hectic day in the Highlands, where the tradition of churchgoing was strong and most Sabbath activity was considered tainted with sin. Whatever bees the police had in their bonnets were unlikely to swarm. In preparation for the arrival of Geordie next day to redecorate his study, he set about moving his entire office to a table at one end of his sitting room. Once his computer and monitor, his printer and fax machine were connected up and his books and files, floppies and CDs were arranged to hand, he was ready. As little more than a test for the new connections, he opened his email.

May Largs, it seemed, must have sat up for half the night, sketching a draft layout for Julian's garden, roughly after the style of the one next door. The uncommonly long time taken for her email to arrive was explained when he found that she had attached several pages of sketches. Even a first glance suggested that the final result would be exactly what he had hoped for. The planting was indicated not by specifics but by generalities – *Ground cover, blue, vinca major?* was a typical notation. The hedge was maintained but a cleverly sited archway (closed only by inconspicuous chicken wire) would allow those in each garden a glimpse of the other, thus suggesting double the space. A cost, inclusive of fees, work and planting, was described as approximate. It was not a small sum but it would still be within his means and he would spend it gladly. He emailed back, requesting a more detailed design and quotation and agreeing to the quoted fee.

The only other item was headed *Friendly Warning*. The message read *Let the cause of the fatal accident rest. You have nothing to gain and you will do the girl more harm than good*. It was unsigned. The *From* line only contained an incomprehensible jumble of letters and numerals followed by the acronym of one of the very largest service providers.

He drove into Tain for some shopping to replenish his larder but the rest of the day dribbled away in dreams of a remodelled garden and in preparing the spare bedroom for Geordie's attention when the study was finished. Between times, he puzzled over the origin, meaning and intent of the email. If it was a genuinely threatening message, which seemed questionable, the police might be able to track it back to its originator. If news of his enquiries had come back to the dangerous driver who had caused the fatal accident, that person might be trying to choke him off. But the spurious tip-off to the journalist seemed to have a more far ranging implication. It meant nothing that the writer had access to a computer and the Internet – in this age of the cybercafe and with schools and colleges cluttered with computers, anyone with the merest smattering of computer literacy could have managed it. There was nothing to be deduced from the fact that the sender knew of his enquiries. Dean Murray's parents would certainly have gossiped about his visit. Use of his email address was more worrying, but it might be that accidental exposure of the address had suggested the email. Whatever the background, he had no intention of leaving Dell in the lurch.

Next morning he awoke convinced that the spell of quiet would be over. New Zealand would have done a day's work already. But there was nothing in the email and still no approach from the Criminal Investigation arm of the law.

He had to quit the Internet in order to make his morning call to Delia. He really must get another telephone line, he told himself. The ward phones must have been busy because he suffered an apparently endless delay before Delia at last came on the line. On reflection, he had decided that Delia had quite enough to worry about without being burdened with his disquieting hunches so he said nothing about the email and gave her no details of his talk with Mr

Maclure.

Delia reported that she was mending satisfactorily but she was restless. Hospital staff, she said, kept telling her that she would be allowed 'home', probably by the next weekend. This was all very well and good, but where was home? There was nowhere that she thought of as home any more and however much money she possessed in theory she did not, in practice, have even the coins that Julian had left with her because she had spent most of them on newspapers, trying to absorb whatever was important in the country that had given her life but which she had never seen since she was out of nappies. There was a catch in her voice. He told her to relax. He would ensure that she had somewhere to lay her head and was not put out into the street to starve. Warmth came back into her voice as she loaded her thanks on to him.

Without giving her cause to panic he tried, very tactfully, to enquire whether there was any unusual circumstance in connection with her money, other than the fact that she could not get her hands on it. He drew a blank. She and her brother had sold the family farm and deposited the money where

116

the family had banked for years. Full stop. Her only surviving relatives in Scotland, so far as she knew, were the cousins near Glasgow whom she had not seen since she was three years old. They had never exchanged even a Christmas card. When Delia and her brother had been preparing for their transfer to the UK she had sent a post card to a possibly outdated address in Falkirk but had received no reply.

When the call had finished, he asked himself what he thought he was getting into. His remit was to establish her identity and obtain her funds and her inheritance, nothing more than that. Gradually, perhaps unwittingly on her part, he was being coaxed into taking her under his wing.

While he was on the phone, the drought of mail had become a flood. The postman had visited – he heard the rattle of the letterbox and the soft thump of letters on the doormat. Almost all of it was junk mail. His name had already found its way on to several mailing lists and the trickle was becoming a flood. Even Dell must have got on to at least one mailing list because a plant and seed catalogue was addressed to her. Her name and his address must have escaped thanks to

May Largs's efforts. He began work on the insurance claim form, laying emphasis on the probability that the driver had been run off the road by an overloaded van. The photographs might help but – a most un-lawyer-like thought – if the insurers proved obdurate Dell should be well able to afford the loss of the price of one car.

He was interrupted by the telephone. The caller was Mr Fasque of the Highlands and Islands Bank. He would be free to visit Miss Barrow in hospital that afternoon. Could Mr Custer attend? Remembering that he wanted several signatures and some information from Delia, Julian decided that the journey would be worthwhile. He said that he certainly could. They agreed a time.

The clock told him that he had time to get to Inverness and to lunch at North Kessock on the way. He even had a few extra minutes in hand. He logged on again, reminding himself again that he must get at least one more telephone landline installed and to check when broadband would be available in his remote area. Another email had come in. Hudson and Larks expressed shock and sorrow at the news of the death of one of their clients and confirmed that they held the will and testament of Aloysius Barrow. It appeared that neither Miss Barrow nor her brother had used the bank's credit card. Lacking any other credit card, she would have to establish her identity in some other way. They had consulted an expert who had confirmed that the letter of appointment was indeed in the handwriting of Delia Barrow and they would be happy to deliver the original of the will as soon as their account (attached) was settled, but in the meantime they could confirm that Miss Barrow would be the principal and residual legatee of her brother. There was, however, a snag. (Julian nodded to himself. There was always a snag. How else would lawyers make a living?) It seemed that Aloysius Barrow had named his sister as his executor, a perfectly legal move but one that was bound to arouse suspicions in the minds of the police. The writer remained vague as to why this was a snag, but Julian could well see without being told that approaches to the lawyers by the police would suggest that there were questions attached to Aloysius Barrow's death that would make it unwise to release her brother's legacy to her until the cause of his death was officially determined.

Julian made a face that scared a sparrow off his window sill where it had been looking for his usual gift of crumbs. He had made up his mind that he was not going to advance money to Miss Barrow until he had something on account, but if that resolution was not to go by the board he would soon have to obtain access for her at least to her own money even if her late brother's remained out of reach for the moment.

He was careful to arrive at Delia's bedside with time in hand. His client was out of bed and sitting, well cushioned, in a hard-looking hospital 'fireside' chair in an otherwise unoccupied TV room at the end of the ward. Julian accepted an even harder-looking visitor's chair. Although dressings and a cast were in evidence Julian was pleased to see her for the first time other than prone. This improvement in her state, the arrival of one visitor and the prospect of another were sufficient to explain a definite upswing in her mood. For the first time, she was seeing Julian properly dressed and on his feet and with her mind unclouded by the aftermath of concussion. He looked younger than her first impression, fit and slightly tanned, although to have qualified as a solicitor and gained the amount of experience that he exhibited meant that he could not be the youth that his appearance suggested to her. He was of medium height and slim – indeed it passed through her mind that he needed feeding up. He wore his dark hair slightly long for a man of the law, but it stayed in place because of a natural wave that she rather envied. His eyes were clear and honest and his face ... After some thought she was still unable to attach any label to it except *likeable*, which, she decided, was quite good enough for the moment though if she decided to correspond with her friends in New Zealand she would have to arrive at a more fulsome description. She also decided, by some intuitive means, that he was very shy. She signed the forms without any quibble and her signatures were witnessed by the ward sister and a nurse.

For his part, Julian was seeing his client for the first time on the road to recovery. The realization that something was in actuality happening at last towards the resolution of her problems, together with the certainty that Julian would be able to cut the Gordian knot, had combined to relax her and to bring animation to her face and colour to her cheeks. Looking at her afresh, Julian decided that she was not a bad-looking sort of girl. The fact that she was regarding him with trust bordering on affection may have influenced his judgement in this respect. She noticed that one of his dressings was loose and while she tucked it in for him she admired his remaining scars. He listened to an account of her progress towards recovery.

They got down to business at last. 'Tell me,' he said, 'do you intend to settle down in the Highlands?'

The question puzzled her. Could he already be thinking in terms of a lasting relationship? The prospect was strangely exciting. 'I expect so,' she said. 'I wouldn't go back to New Zealand now. Too many memories! I don't know anybody up here – except you and Mrs Campbell – but there may be people who remember my family. Why do you ask?'

'There are indeed people who remember your family. I was speaking to a farmer and his wife yesterday who remembered several of your aunts and uncles. They could make a guess as to which branch of the family your cousins in the Glasgow area belonged to and they think that you may have some more cousins living in the Brora area. But I asked the question because if you settle anywhere except in a city, you're bound to need a driving licence at some time. Have you ever held one?'

'I had a New Zealand licence.'

'Presumably it burned with the rest of your papers. You passed your test in New Zealand?'

She nodded. Great! A British citizen whose overseas licence had been destroyed. Perhaps Hudson and Larks could be induced to earn their fee after all. He obtained as many details as she could remember.

The right moment seemed to have arrived for him to tell her, very gently, that the Highland Police had been in touch with New Zealand, enquiring into such matters as her finances. She took it calmly, apparently accepting that the movement of large sums of money was bound to cause ripples in the legal pond. It was too early to start her worrying about the inferences that hostile officialdom might draw.

Mr Fasque arrived precisely at the appointed hour and before Julian could warn her to guard her tongue. He was a middle-aged man, putting on some weight and showing it in his high colour. He was dressed as bank managers used to dress, in a black jacket, stiff collar and striped trousers with a modest flower in his buttonhole and the corners of a handkerchief showing in his breast pocket. That alone would have suggested to Julian, if he had not already known it, that the man was a fusspot. However, he did greet Miss Barrow in a friendly manner and by that name, and he seemed genuinely concerned as he enquired after her recovery. Julian gave him his chair and fetched from the ward another that he found to be even less comfortable.

Mr Fasque seemed more concerned but in a very different manner when Julian produced printouts of his correspondence with Hudson and Larks. Oh dear no! He could hardly recommend the release of a substantial sum of money, two substantial sums in fact, on the basis of an identification that so far was supported only by a facsimile of handwriting and the personal statement of the party concerned. He was happy to certify that the photographs handed to him by Mr Custer were true and accurate representations of the young lady who had been introduced to him as Delia Barrow, but beyond that point he could not be budged. If she could produce a passport, say, or a birth certificate or even a driving licence...

'You know as well as I do,' Julian said in as reasonable a tone as he could manage, 'that a copy birth certificate is only a formality, but one which may take long enough. A replacement passport may take twice as long after that. Even then, the issuing authorities will have had no more to go on than you already do, other than the original photographs in the passport office. Here you have evidence that these photographs were recognized by friends and lawyers in New Zealand. What more could you possibly want?'

Mr Fasque pursed his tight, pink lips. 'You know what I want. I want some official backing before I open the door on such large sums of money. Ideally, I would like a court to confirm the young lady's identity.'

'So would I. And in due course that may have to be arranged. Perhaps you would make a note that when Miss Barrow receives her money she would be pleased to receive a visit from the bank's investment adviser. For the moment, a bridging loan would suffice.'

This hint at stability had only a slightly

mollifying effect on Mr Fasque. 'I could hardly agree to lend money to somebody who is only a face to me, without any security at all. Of course, if you cared to act as guarantor...'

Julian felt his sphincter snap shut. He had become satisfied as to Delia's identity but not necessarily as to her *bona fides* and most particularly not while the police were asking pointed questions. He liked Delia and was inclined to trust her but, as any solicitor knows, the most likeable and apparently reliable person is as likely as anyone else to default. A fellow solicitor and former fellow student had agreed to act as guarantor of a loan and the borrower, a friendly man of open and honest manner, instead of completing the purchase of the property had drawn the money and fled abroad leaving his unfortunate backer to pay off the loan by means of a substantial mortgage on his own house.

Delia, without even glancing at him, came to his relief. 'I wouldn't think of it,' she said. 'Mr Custer doesn't know me from a can of fish and the situation is much as he said. There has to be another way.'

Julian's deliberations had born fruit. 'There

is,' he said. 'It will take time to get you access to the two bank accounts, but we can keep you solvent by another means. Mr Fasque's bank has been issuing its own credit card, under the banner of Master Card, for some years now. He can issue you a platinum card on the strength of these emails. That would enable you to buy some clothes and to subsist until I can get him or a court to recognize your identity.'

Mr Fasque sat up very straight and his voice rose. 'Just a ... a minute,' he squeaked. Julian had the impression that he had nearly uttered a rude word. 'That amounts to the same thing.'

As clearly as if he had direct telepathic communication with Mr Fasque, Julian knew that Mr Fasque was aware of the enquiries by the police. He also knew that credit cards are issued with little or no enquiry into the *bona fides* of the applicant. If time had allowed he would have been tempted to apply for a credit card in the name, say, of Bonzo Campbell and then to use that as a lever in argument. But perhaps the threat would suffice. 'Quite right,' he said. 'But of course the sums involved will be very much smaller. And of course I can't make you. But if you don't I shall have a selection of my friends and clients make applications for credit cards in the names of their household pets. That will keep your organization busy while I go straight to the nearest Clydesdale or Royal Bank. You know how easily they issue credit cards these days – especially if the very sizeable account of the holder will follow it. Which it will. And if that happens I will make sure that your head office knows how you came to lose that account.'

'But that would take just as long...' Mr Fasque protested.

Julian leaned forward and held his eye. 'Not necessarily, and you know it. The process of issuing a credit card takes only minutes, it is only the office procedures that take a little time. I expect you to go from here back to your office and send some junior here with the application form, to be signed in his presence and brought back to your office for immediate processing. I expect the card to have an expenditure limit of not less than ten thousand pounds. And I expect the card to be issued within three days.'

'Even Clydesdale couldn't do it within that time,' Mr Fasque protested.

'I think they could. But unless I have your assurance, I shall go home and use the Internet to find somebody who can. With the promise of an account this size to follow, I expect no difficulty. And the rest of my outline stands.'

'But she has no permanent address.'

'Make it care of the bank. Or care of me, if you prefer.'

Mr Fasque threw up his hands and uttered a cry of pain. It was improper. It was unprecedented. It was quite impossible.

When Mr Fasque had gone on his way, still protesting, Delia said, 'Wow! I'd no idea that you could be such a tiger. Bullying a bank manager like that ... Will he do it?'

'He'll do it. He won't want head office to find that he's thrown away the chance of such a large account.'

'I hope you're right. But he knows that the police are asking questions. If they kick me out of here on Friday, I'll need clothes and somewhere to stay.'

'Don't worry about it,' Julian said. 'I'll find you bed and board somewhere. And if you have money coming, you can always get credit. Did you ever see the film about the million pound note? Never mind. Trust me, you won't starve.'

'And you'll buy me something to wear to leave here in? They had to cut most of my clothes off me while they thought my arm was broken as well as my leg.'

Julian tried not to sigh too ostentatiously. 'Write down your sizes and give me a list,' he said. 'You shall have clothes. I take it that they didn't have to cut your shoes off you? Shoes are the one thing that you have to try on. Nobody else can buy them for you.'

Delia looked surprised. Julian realized that to a woman the appearance of the shoes far outweighs their comfort in importance. 'Shoes are about all I do have,' she said. 'I don't think that Inverness is quite ready for me to walk around the streets in nothing but shoes.'

Julian got away as soon as he could. A female client who made suggestive remarks while regarding him with the look of an adoring spaniel was rather too much to cope with. He considered walking into the right sort of shop and handing over Dell's list of sizes. He could describe her style and colouring and tell the assistant 'Put together a complete wardrobe for a lady of this colouring.' But she would be sure to ask embarrassing questions to which he would not have the faintest idea of the answers. She would think that he was clothing a mistress. Or, worse, that he was a transvestite.

Nine

Looking back later, Julian was hard put to it to remember what individual tasks had turned his week from an interval of leisure into a period of frantic constant activity. He had lost most of Monday to his visit to Delia and Friday had to be earmarked for fetching her; but where had the intervening three days vanished? He had intended to get on with setting his house in order, keeping Geordie busy with the redecoration while he attended to carpets, curtains and the arrangement of furniture. But some of those very people and bodies who he had expected, with a confidence born of experience, to mess him about and keep him waiting while he badgered them by phone and email now moved with extraordinary and inconvenient promptness. The photographs, properly attested, arrived from New Zealand. The replacement birth certificate also turned up. On the other hand, the processes of applying for passport and driving licence, on behalf of a hospital patient with dual nationality, no documents and no fixed abode, proved to be long-winded and complex.

The procurator fiscal had decided that a fatal accident enquiry would not be appropriate, since there was no doubt whatever as to how the driver had died and a death certificate had been issued accordingly. Nevertheless, he seemed to be in no hurry to release the body for burial. It suited Julian very well to postpone any question of a funeral until Delia, the only real mourner available, was out of hospital and sufficiently recovered to stand and kneel. Julian prepared an application for a court hearing at which Dell could speak up for herself and be declared the one and only genuine Delia Barrow, sister and executor of Aloysius Barrow deceased, but he held it in reserve. If the onward course of events resulted in her recognition by the various branches of officialdom, that would be quite satisfactory though there would remain the risk of a later challenge by some claimant to the money. Although relatives to the Barrow siblings seemed to be remote and uninterested, it was Julian's experience that where large sums of money are concerned there are always claimants.

Delia's new credit card, issued by the Highlands and Islands Bank, also arrived, but the Highlands and Islands bank was not yet so up-to-date as no longer to require her signature, accepting, as did other banks, the secret PIN number. Thus Julian could not use it and, when he and Grace made a shopping expedition to Dingwall, he had to use his own to purchase what Grace swore was the absolute, irreducible minimum of clothes and make-up necessary to get Delia out of Raigmore without being arrested or pilloried. And so his first resolution, not to lend her money or to incur debts on her behalf, went by the board.

By the Thursday, when he thought that he had broken the back of Delia's problems, written the last statement, sent the last email and had the last angry telephone argument with some obstructive civil servant, he realized with a shock that Delia was due to be released the following day. Comfortable in the knowledge that the Dornoch area was well provided with hotels and B&Bs, he had done nothing about accommodation for her. Due to Geordie's efforts and his own, Julian's house was in no state for a visitor, being half stripped of paper, encumbered with pots of paint and wallpaper paste and much of the furniture crammed into what should have been the spare room. Moreover, he was far from sure what Delia's reaction would be if she were offered bed and board unchaperoned in the house of a bachelor lawyer. He had an impression that New Zealand remained rather strait-laced; on the other hand, farming communities were usually less trammelled. He had had hopes of Geordie's sister Hilda, but his own sudden demand for Geordie's services had left their small house in a similar barely habitable state, while Grace was expecting an elderly aunt to visit and take occupation of her only spare bedroom.

Julian spent an hour that he could hardly spare on the telephone, only to find that accommodation was at a premium. A major golf tournament was being held in Dornoch that weekend, attracting the usual high attendance from Europe and America. The tourist season was beginning. The available hotel and bed-and-breakfast rooms were fully booked. Yet he was determined that Delia must be lodged nearby. He could have found her accommodation in Inverness, but she would have known nobody there and the difficulty of client conferences would have been trebled.

Any mention of Canmore House Hotel during these phone-calls had produced a variety of responses, but the overall burden of them had been that Canmore House was out of commission and likely to remain so. It seemed to Julian that an empty hotel (only two miles away as the crow flew although ten or twelve by road, whichever way you circled the Firth) must surely be able to produce one empty room for an old friend. From the depths of sometimes bitter experience, he knew that it is easier to deny such a possibility over the telephone than face to face when the enquirer can see for himself how the land lies. He cast one apologetic glance at his computer, where the third draft of his court application was languishing in the word processor program and two unanswered emails waited in the in-tray; but somewhere for Delia to lay her head took precedence. He drove off clockwise around the Firth. Looking south from the other side of the Dornoch Firth, he could make out the group of three houses huddled together, bright against the dark conifers that drape the hillsides of Easter Ross.

The Canmore House Hotel had been built as a mansion for one of the premier families of the region, but between dwindling family sizes and an inherited inability to judge the stamina of horses it had become too large and expensive for its purpose and by early in the twentieth century had become a very upmarket hotel. The dignity of the stone and slate building with its carefully tended cladding of flowering climbers was spoiled for the moment by the coming and going of men in variously coloured overalls, the litter of builders' materials and equipment and two skips overflowing with discarded materials; but nothing could diminish the beauty of the gardens. These, looking as though God and nature had worked hand in hand, bore the imprint, unmistakable to those who know about such matters, of May Largs. Julian decided that Derek McTaggart, the manager and part proprietor, must be suffering agonies of frustration at having the place lying empty.

Attached to the back of the hotel, in a wing that had once been stables, was a small house. Derek McTaggart emerged from the house door as Julian pulled up at the front. Derek had put on weight but Julian knew him immediately. The two had been friends at University and recognition was mutual.

Derek hurried forward to shake hands. 'Come inside,' he said. 'I heard that you were back. You've bought the house next door to Grace Campbell?'

'Yes. You know her?'

'We were at school together. Come into the house. Nobody should see the inside of the hotel, the state it's in. I was going to phone you.' With this apparent *non sequitur* he led the way indoors and into a sitting room that was surprisingly smart and modern considering the signs of devastation outside. 'You'll take coffee? Or a dram?'

'Neither, thank you. I'm in the middle of a desperately busy day. What were you going to phone me about?'

'I'll tell you. I need help and advice. I've been an idiot.' (Julian wondered how many first approaches from a client had begun in

137

this manner and decided that he had lost count.) 'And,' Derek said, 'the only solicitor I've ever dealt with around here has a secretary I wouldn't trust to hold her tongue. I don't want this to get around. You know that we had all our piping stolen?'

'I heard. And I could see some of the consequences outside.'

'You heard that they'd stolen all our lead piping?'

Julian looked at his old friend in surprise. It seemed to be an unnecessary repetition. 'That's what I heard.'

'Well, it isn't true. Let me tell you a little history. Britain was lucky, in that the Cornish mines were rich in tin. Tin is still used in large quantities for plating and for alloys. It's imported nowadays, mostly from South America. But there was a time when we were mining more than we needed. The price fell until tin was as cheap as lead. Even then, it was known that tin was also less toxic than lead. The then Marquis of Tain, who owned a lot of the land around here, had big holdings in the Cornish mines and he pushed for the use of tin piping. It didn't catch on much but a few houses were built that way.'

'Including this one?'

'Yes. And when I say tin I don't mean tin-plating like they sell food in. I mean solid metallic tin, used in much the same way as they used lead. I knew about it but I never said anything. I didn't want the place ripped apart, just as it has been. Rather than face the disruption, I preferred to think of it as a reserve against a rainy day. So when this happened, my first instinct was to shut up about it and let it be thought that only lead pipes had been stolen.'

'That was shutting the stable door, wasn't it?' Julian said. 'The pipes had gone.'

They were alone in the house but Derek looked around to be sure. 'The pipes had gone, yes. But what I don't want anyone to know, and I say this very reluctantly even to you, is that sheet tin was used for large areas of the roofs. You look up and see slates, but that's only a small part of it. The flats, the flashings, the valley gutters, they're all pure tin. There's many times more tin up there than the thieves got away with. But on the spur of the moment I told the police and my insurers that they'd only got away with lead.'

'Oh dear!' Julian said without emphasis.

'That's putting it very mildly. Now that I've calmed down and had time to think about it, I can see that the sensible thing would have been to tell the police the truth, make an insurance claim for pure tin piping, sell the tin off the roofs, replace it with lead or one of these modern substitutes and spend the balance on the next phase of refurbishment. But now how do I explain? I misled the police. And will my insurers believe me when I add a small fortune to the amount of my claim?'

This, to Julian, was an old, old story. He hid his amusement. 'To put it bluntly, you want to hide behind me while I make your explanations for you?'

Derek smiled weakly. 'Blunt or not, that's the way of it. Can you dig me out of the hole without spreading the news around?'

'Let me think for a minute.' Julian did so. The first thought that he came out with was, 'I'll take that dram that you offered me while I think some more.' Derek rose and poured a large Glenmorangie. 'Point One,' Julian said. 'Do you have any proof that your pipes were tin?'

'When I suspected it, two years ago, I got a surveyor's report.'

'Good. Point Two. I think we can keep it quiet over the weekend but after that the news will have to be in the public domain. Get your builder here on Monday morning and tell him to get on with stripping the roofs and replacing the tin with anything else you like. Tarpaulins would do for the moment, but I've heard about those lead substitutes. Let's get all that sheet tin into a lock-up. I'll find out about metal dealers – and the proper price to put in your insurance claim. And I'll break the news to the police and your insurers. How's Joan?'

Derek blinked at him in surprise at the change of subject. 'She's fine. At the shops. Why?'

'I was wondering whether she'd object to a female guest in your spare bedroom.'

'I don't suppose she would, in normal times.' Derek lifted his arms and let them fall in a gesture of helplessness. 'We have two spare bedrooms. But with the hotel invaded by workmen I had to move all the silver, the glassware, the pictures and all the more valuable wines, spirits and ornaments into them. I'm sorry, but it's impossible.'

'And you couldn't make one of the hotel bedrooms habitable?'

Derek gave vent to a hollow laugh. 'Not a hope in hell. You don't realize what a mess the thieves left behind. And my builder has to have access to every room. He has to replace all the pipes in copper and restore all the plasterwork and panelling. If his men get turned away because your guest is powdering her nose, the builder has a claim against me for extra time; and, believe me, it costs.' He paused and looked quizzically at his old friend. 'Joan will kick my balls in if I don't find out who this mysterious guest would have been.'

'Just a client.' Julian finished his whisky. 'Never mind. I'll help you all the same.' As he left the house and settled in his driving seat, a thin rain was beginning; but he was grinning to himself all the same. He could see a faint possibility that certain things might after all make sense.

Back at *Pog,* Julian made two phone calls and then spoke to Geordie, who was busily painting a wall in the study. 'Just finish that wall, Geordie, and then come and give me a hand. We'll have to clear a bedroom for Miss Barrow, and if everything has to be piled two deep in the other spare room, that's too bad.'

While Geordie was washing out the roller and closing up paint cans, Julian went up into the attic. This was a haunt of spiders and a repository for the dust of ages, but without getting too dirty or breathing in more than a very little of the dust he managed to scrape a sample off one of the water-pipes. He rather thought that *Pog* had been built later than the Canmore House and thus would not have been one of the houses influenced by the eccentric Marquis of Tain, but it would cost little to find out for sure.

Ten

The rain had passed by during the morning and Julian set off through sunshine pleasantly diffused by thin cloud and a countryside newly washed and refreshed. The hills were softened in outline by a mist that came rolling lazily down the clefts in the hillsides. He had hoped to have Grace with him. Another woman might have proved reassuring to one who was emerging into an unfamiliar land where she had no friends, no support and, for the moment, no money. For all Delia knew, he could have been preparing to sell her into the white slave trade or to be made into meat pies. But Grace had had clients to attend and Julian knew from experience that his own manner, when he troubled to employ it, could usually be relied on to soothe old ladies and nervous animals. That, he thought, should be good enough for a bereaved New Zealander with wealth in prospect.

Traffic was light for once and he was running over the suspension bridge and into Inverness in less than an hour. He tackled the hospital's roundabout system and parked as near as he could manage to the main doors. After delivering the parcel containing Delia's new clothes to her ward he retreated down to keep an appointment in A and E. There, his dressings were removed for the last time and he was pronounced recovered. His skin was still tender but the discomfort was acceptable and soon forgotten except for an occasional itch. He told himself that an itch was a sign of healing and kept reminding himself not to scratch.

Delia, he discovered, was being given a

final examination and a lecture on how to progress without aggravating any of her healing injuries. The world of medicine, he knew only too well, rolls along at its own pace, unhurried and unhurryable and totally unconcerned with the pressures on the timetables of patients. Lawyers, he also knew, are often cast in much the same mould although he always tried to be considerate in this respect. In the certainty that others would not be so considerate, it was his habit never to go for an appointment with a doctor or a fellow lawyer without one book in his briefcase, often two and occasionally three. He returned to the entrance hall, found a seat and settled down for a good read, but for once his book failed to hold his attention and he found his mind arranging and rearranging the facts and possibilities.

When Dell arrived by wheelchair at last, she was clasping an armful of flowers. 'These came by Interflora,' she said. 'They're from friends in New Zealand. I left a whole lot more in the ward, but these were just too beautiful to leave behind. Can we manage them?'

He was surprised at the pleasure he derived from seeing her again but all that he could find to say was, 'I suppose so.'

Delia handed him the flowers. When decanted beside his car, she stood up with the aid of two sticks and lowered herself carefully into the passenger seat. He decided that he would have had no difficulty recognizing the choice of dress as being Grace's. It was as if Grace herself had been trundled through the foyer, but with a less serene expression on the surmounting face. Grace, for all her lively and sometimes ribald sense of humour, carried with her a dignity – stateliness, her husband called it – and this carried over into her taste in clothes. The smart but rather severe frock in grey linen must have had a similar effect on Delia, because she greeted Julian primly, shook hands and thanked him politely for all his help. She then demanded to be carried immediately into the shopping area of Inverness.

Julian had little time to spare for a shopping expedition. He explained that Delia's new credit card would be of no use to her until she was apprised of her PIN number. She retorted that the small sealed envelope had been delivered by hand the previous day and she had no intention of going around dressed like a schoolteacher in mourning. Moreover, she did not have a clean change of *anything*.

Julian spared a moment to wish that Mr Fasque had not so suddenly forsaken his obstructive habit and leaped to her aid. He still refused to go into Inverness, where parking is almost impossible and there are too many shops. It was his experience that any lady released into such an environment with a credit card would disappear for hours, possibly for ever. Dornoch, on the other hand, had limited shopping for the lady in need of a whole new wardrobe and Tain was little better. Searching quickly for a town with good parking and just the right number of shops, his memory threw up Dingwall, which was almost on their route home.

In Dingwall, he pulled into one of the peripheral car parks. Delia was disappointed when he refused to accompany her as critic and porter. She argued that Ally would certainly have done so, but when he got out his laptop and began composing a statement for the police on the subject of solid tin piping she accepted that he was a busy man with other calls on his time. She set off into the circuit of shopping streets, limping and leaning on her sticks but definitely not to be deterred.

He had finished his statement, made two calls on his cellphone and resumed reading his book before she returned, just within the time that he had set for her. She was burdened with many parcels confined for the moment in a cheap rucksack. She had the purged look of a woman who has had the run of the shops. He knew of a small restaurant not far away and he took her there for a late and hasty lunch.

'You've never told me where I'm going to be staying,' she said suddenly.

The waitress, arriving with their main course, gained him time to compose himself. He thought that it had taken Delia a long time to get around to asking the question. 'I met with a problem,' he said. 'There's a golf tournament on, and one major hotel isn't ready to reopen. You'll be staying in my house.'

She accepted the news with a blink and a look into his face that he found difficult to interpret, but then she smiled. 'That's good of you,' she said. 'Don't forget to make a charge for it in your final account. I'll try not to get in your way.'

He was careful not to show surprise. He supposed that New Zealand might be less strait-laced than he had thought and much less so than the Scottish Highlands. It never occurred to him that Delia had been very much impressed by his courtesy. He was certainly a cut above the workers on the sheep station. To her, he was the epitome of the British gentleman. She could picture him in a bowler hat. She was not in the least afraid of being molested by him, because her daydreams had begun to incorporate certain incidents of respectful molestation that might not have shocked him but would certainly have startled him out of his wits.

'And I'll try not to get in yours,' he said. 'You don't mind the smell of paint?'

'No. Why?'

'We're in the middle of redecorating,' he apologized.

'Who's we?' she asked quickly.

'Just me and the neighbour who's helping me out.'

He insisted that the bill for their meal be brought with the sweet course. 'Why the hurry?' she asked plaintively

'I've arranged to meet that traffic policeman this afternoon, the one who attended at the scene of your crash.'

'The cute one?' she asked, laughing.

'That,' he said, 'is a matter of opinion. But he couldn't promise me a time. And in my experience, the moment you finish your meal everybody disappears. When you do manage to get the bill they vanish again. If you ever manage to pay the bill they disappear again, leaving you to wonder when, if ever, you'll get your credit card back or your change.'

Delia made a mental note for future use. 'Why do you want to see him?' she asked. 'Or does he want to see you?'

'I want to see him. You'll understand why when you hear what I have to say. Mostly I want to pump him about what his superiors are thinking.'

She nodded. 'Ally was just the same,' she said comfortably. 'He hated to tell the same story more than once.'

He let her lean on him, back to the car. She certainly tried to be accommodating. It was as if this was her home country now. She looked around with renewed interest as he drove, asking questions about the people and the places, most particularly the agriculturc. She noticed when they rejoined the main road and again when they left it. The wild scenery of the short cut over the hills seemed to impress her. When the view over Dornoch Firth opened up, she said that it was very like parts of New Zealand. He was illogically pleased that the sun had been shining on her first view of his home territory.

She also admired his house. Julian noticed that she made excuses to hobble through all the rooms – looking, he thought, for signs of another woman but she only found Geordie. She expressed satisfaction with her room, even in its partially decorated state, and set about unpacking her shopping into the hastily emptied cupboards, refusing his offer of help. He left her to get on with it. When PC Weigh phoned to say that he would join them within about five minutes, Julian called to her from the study. She joined him in the kitchen in a more colourful blouse and skirt, a summery combination in cheerful colours that brought life to her appearance. He felt that he was seeing her for the first time. For a moment, something warm and magical leaped between them.

'You don't mind?' she asked anxiously.

'Mind what?' He busied himself making tea.

'That I've changed out of the dress you bought for me. I'm more a jeans sort of person. I didn't want to hurt your feelings and I thought that maybe that was how one was expected to dress around here.'

He laughed. 'I didn't choose that dress. Grace Campbell picked it out. I asked her to do the shopping for me. I'd have made terrible mistakes. But do I gather that she didn't do much better? Her style is certainly much more severe than yours.'

'I suppose,' she said fairly, 'that Mrs Campbell had never seen me dressed and on my feet, so she didn't have much to go on. She chose the undies too?'

He felt himself turning pink. 'Good God, yes.'

She smiled in relief. 'That's all right then. You can tell a lot about what a man thinks of a girl by the undies he buys for her.'

So she was more sophisticated than he had thought. He was straying on to dangerous territory but he could not help being curious. 'Have men often bought you lingerie?' He felt the heartbeat of anxiety.

'Sometimes.' She hurried to explain but

152

without looking coy or even blushing. 'Not as a present but for me in the sense of doing my shopping for me. The sheep station was away out in the hills. Sometimes I made my own, but if one of the men was going into town and I couldn't spare the time to go with him I'd give him a note and sizes and colours but what he brought back was usually more his idea of me than mine.'

'More frivolous or more sober?' he asked, laughing. 'No, you'd better not answer that, but you do look about a thousand per cent better than I've ever seen you do before.'

She lit up. 'Is that right?'

Somehow the idea of other men picturing her *en déshabillé* was upsetting. He was struggling to find some very different topic when he was saved by the arrival of Constable Weigh at the door. They settled in the sitting room. Here, decoration had progressed no further than changing one wall to the colour of sunshine on dead bracken, which clashed seriously with the institutional green of the unaltered walls. Julian saw Delia avert her eyes. He dispensed tea and biscuits.

'I wanted to see you,' Weigh said. 'My superiors want to ask Miss Barrow some questions. I was under orders to tell them when you'd be home, so you should be hearing from them soon.'

'We will make them welcome. I wanted a word with you,' Julian told the constable, 'because I was consulted by Mr McTaggart at the Canmore House Hotel. I want Miss Barrow to hear this because I think it connects with her accident.

'Mr McTaggart feels that he's been foolish. You may be able to help me to get him out of his folly without too many repercussions. When the piping was stolen, he panicked. It wasn't just lead that was stolen, it was the much more valuable tin. Not tinplate but solid, metallic tin. He'd known for some time that solid tin had been used instead of lead at the time when the hotel was built. He didn't want that fact to be generally known and in a moment of panic he allowed you and his insurers to go on thinking of lead. Part of his problem now is the realization that there is also a great deal of tin in the roofing of the hotel and it seems likely that somebody knows about it. Rather than risk waking up one morning with all his roofs stripped he wants to make a clean breast of it now. I've written you out a report. Here's a printout.'

PC Weigh read rapidly through the two pages and nodded. 'Very cautiously worded,' he said. 'You convey the facts without leaving the door open for criticism of your client. That seems to cover it.'

'Not by a mile,' said Julian. 'Something else occurred to me while I was talking with Mr McTaggart. Tin isn't quite as heavy as lead, but it's heavy enough. It would be a fair bet that at least one of the thieves worked for the firm of builders. They probably took the piping away on one of the firm's lorries. Imagine two or three inexperienced men. They start loading the van with ingots of tin. They don't realize how much they're putting into it. The innocent – in the classical sense of ignorant – Dean Murray has been recruited as driver and possibly as lookout. He drives off. When he arrives at the main road, he doesn't have a hope in hell of making such a sharp turn with such a load on board. Then, having had a near collision and seeing the crash in his mirrors, he realizes that he's in trouble. Dangerous driving resulting in a fatality, although he doesn't know about the fatality yet; overloading a vehicle and, of course, being in possession of a stolen and valuable, perhaps almost semi-precious

155

metal. He decides to scram and lie low until it's blown over.'

'That's exactly how it looked,' Delia exclaimed. 'Your explanation brought it back. The picture's quite clear in my mind. The van trying to turn the corner but being dragged sideways, not by the speed but by the load in it.'

PC Weigh was shaking his head. 'Coming from Canmore House Hotel, he'd have been going the other way.'

'The hotel was robbed a week before the accident,' Julian said. 'They'd have spent the time melting the tin down and casting it into ingots. That would make it much more difficult to identify.'

The PC was catching up at his own pace. 'If you're right, we have the solution to two cases in our hands. Dangerous driving resulting in a fatality and the theft of the piping. And now, I'm wondering...?'

Julian could see exactly what was in the constable's mind. 'It's all right,' he said. 'You can take the credit for the idea. But can you help to see that a blind eye gets turned to my foolish client's careless misleading statement to the police?'

'Probably. I can't do better than to mimic

the line you took in your statement.' There was a pause while PC Weigh made notes. 'So they were doing the melting down somewhere along the road that we guessed the van had come out of.'

'And quite close to the main road, or Dean would have noticed that the van was handling like trying to steer a cow by the tail,' said Julian. 'Tell me, does Fergus Donelly live along that road?'

'I don't know,' said the PC. 'But I'll dashed soon find out.' He looked at his watch. 'For the moment, I'll have to leave it. My shift has just ended.'

Eleven minutes to five seemed an unusual time for a change of shift but Julian took the hint. They seemed to have arrived at an understanding that a tot of whisky would seal. Delia turned out also to enjoy a good whisky.

Perhaps because he knew that his seniors could be expected to arrive before long, Constable Weigh accepted only a comparatively modest drink, downed it and made his escape within a few minutes. Dell had only just emerged from hospital and had undertaken a shopping expedition to boot while Julian had alternated driving with mental effort. Each felt in need of rest rather than food. The two relaxed in quiet amity, each afraid to burst their own little bubble of companionship. The bottle of Glenmorangie passed to and fro.

It was some little time before the sound of a car followed by a ring at the doorbell warned of visitors. Julian's first impulse was to let Delia go to answer it; after all, it was Delia who the visitors had come to see. But he had to admit to himself that it was his house and that Delia had an incompletely mended broken leg, so he supposed that it was up to him. He heaved himself to his feet and went to the door. It took a moment of fiddling before he had the door open and during that time the bell rang again.

Two men stood on the doorstep. The taller of the two was closer and so could be assumed to have done the ringing. 'Mr Custer? I'm Detective Inspector Fauldhouse. I'd appreciate a word with you.' His height made him look deceptively thin and his cast of features was ordinary, but his tone was brisk and he spoke as though he expected people to jump at his command. As he spoke he moved forward to cross the threshold.

As a solicitor, Julian had acquired an intense dislike of policemen who had gained delusions of omnipotence from the respect that usually went with the job. 'If you were really a detective,' he said politely, 'you might have worked out that the sound of somebody releasing the chain meant that the door was being answered. It follows as the night follows the day that either you are not a detective or else that you do not have the sense or courtesy to wait for the door to be answered before ringing again. Which would you suggest to be the case?' Julian was always inclined to become grandiloquent in his cups.

Inspector Fauldhouse had ventured this far in person reluctantly. Not many years earlier he had become convinced that Grace Campbell had made away with her husband's appalling old uncle and, indeed, he was still half convinced of it. However, somebody else had been convicted of the crime and was serving a nominal life sentence for it, so in the eyes of the law Mrs Campbell had to be guiltless. Whenever their paths crossed, Mrs Campbell was wont to abandon her dignified posture, greet him with a broad grin and seem to be on the point of granting him a salute with less than the usual number of fingers. Lacking any suitable reply, the inspector had fallen into the habit of avoiding the vicinity of Grace Campbell as though it was infected with the bubonic plague. Now here he was again, wrong-footed and made to look an idiot.

Well aware that Sergeant Ballintore was listening with considerable amusement to his superior being taken down a peg or two, the inspector decided that there was no reply to Julian's question that would not show him in an even worse light. 'Is Miss Barrow here?' he asked gruffly.

'She is.'

'Can we see her, please?'

Rather than make semantic hay with the difference between *can* and *may*, Julian said, 'I will ask her,' and closed the door in the inspector's face.

In the sitting room, 'Could you hear that?' Julian asked.

Delia replaced her glass beside the sadly depleted whisky bottle. She grinned at him. 'Enough. Should I see him now?'

'It's usually better to find out what they're after sooner rather than later.'

'You'll stay with me?'

'Of course. And if I tell you to shut up, you

160

do just that.'

'Got you,' Dell said.

Julian returned to the front door and opened it on the seething inspector. 'You may
come in,' he said. 'Miss Barrow will see you.
Wipe your feet.'

If the cheerful colour of the one wall so far
decorated impressed the inspector, he was
not going to admit it. He took a seat in the
wing-chair indicated by Julian and his sergeant took the other, but when Julian joined
Delia on the settee the inspector objected. 'I
want to see Miss Barrow alone,' he said.

'I expect you do,' Julian said, 'but you're
not going to. I am her solicitor and I stay.'

'Why would you suppose that she needs a
solicitor present?'

The sergeant had been taking notes. Julian
noticed that his pencil had stopped. 'Please
make a note of the inspector's last question,'
Julian told him.

'I withdraw the question.'

'No you don't. If we're having a record
taken, let's make it a complete one.'

There was, in fact, nothing wrong with the
inspector's question. It was a typical example of a not very intelligent officer fishing
for admissions; but the inspector sensed a

trap and chose his words with greater care.

'You are Miss Delia Barrow, late of the Crag Valley Sheep Station, South Island, New Zealand?'

Through lips that seemed to have been frozen stiff, Delia agreed that she was.

'You were the sister of the late Aloysius Barrow, same address?'

'That's me.'

'Would you care to tell me about the accident in which he died.'

Delia looked anxiously at Julian who said, 'Miss Barrow has already made a lengthy statement on the subject. And so have I.'

'Of course, of course,' the inspector said affably. 'But those were simple statements to a road traffic constable. We are looking for a little more depth.'

'With what end in mind?'

'You don't really expect me to answer that question, surely.'

Julian glanced at the sergeant. The pencil was still moving. 'No, I don't. I just wanted to get your evasion of it into the record.' He transferred his eyes to Delia. 'Go ahead,' he told her.

'All right.' Delia paused to gather her thoughts and arrange her words. 'My brother was driving. The car was a two-year-old Ford that we bought in London. We were heading for Croik Castle near Thurso, where my brother was to take up a new post. We had crossed that low bridge over the Dornoch Firth. Suddenly a van came out of a minor road on our right, turning towards us. The driver seemed to be having a hard time pulling it round sharply enough and my brother had to swerve on to the shoulder or hit him. The shoulder there seemed kind of high compared to what I'm used to and the car made a leap. I'd just turned around a minute earlier, to reach something off the back seat, so my seat belt was undone. Otherwise I guess I would have died like my brother. I was thrown out. I cracked a bone in my leg and gave my arm an almighty twist, but I survived. The car burst into flames, but I didn't know that at the time.

'Next I knew I was in an ambulance and Mr Custer here was with me because of his burns. One of the paramedics told me that Mr Custer's a lawyer so I asked him later to help me replace my passport, my birth certificate and all my bank papers.' She paused and looked at the inspector with comical uncertainty. 'Do I tell you about the

163

marks in the road? I only saw photographs.'

'I can speak about those,' Julian said. He felt suddenly sober. 'I arrived on the scene only seconds after the smash. Mrs Campbell was right behind me. I made an abortive attempt to get to the driver of the crashed car, who I now know to have been Aloysius Barrow. As Miss Barrow said, the car burst into flames and I was driven back. Mrs Campbell called the emergency services. They arrived almost immediately. Miss Barrow was attended to and I was taken into the ambulance, but during the interim I had noticed the dark skid marks in the road. They seemed very much as if another vehicle had come out of the side-road which I now know to be the road from Cuthmore and had taken a wide swing, forcing the car driven by Mr Barrow to take to the verge. It looked as if the other vehicle had been going too fast to make the turn, but I later learned that –'

'Please stick to what you know of your own knowledge,' said the inspector.

'All right. I suggested to Mrs Campbell that she use my camera to record the marks. Copies of those photographs and of others that she took of the crash site are in the possession of the traffic department.'

'Thank you.' The inspector turned his attention back to Delia, who moistened her lips. 'Miss Barrow, is it not true that you were the passenger in a car that crashed in New Zealand in not dissimilar circumstances, with fatal consequences.'

'I don't think that you should answer that,' Julian said. 'It's not relevant and discussion of the similarity or otherwise of the circumstances can lead us even further afield. I would certainly want first to ask Miss Barrow about any such incident, in order to find out what similarities there were between the circumstances surrounding the two mishaps.'

The inspector seemed not the least put out. 'Very well,' he said. 'Miss Barrow, you did a lot of driving in New Zealand, didn't you?'

'Yes. Everyone has to if they live well off the beaten track, as I did.'

'You were in one or two accidents?'

'Two. We had fifteen kilometres of unsealed road leading up to the station. It was very rough and twisting with a loose surface. Everybody had accidents.'

'Miss Barrow, is it not true that you had a

history of quarrelling with your brother?'

Julian looked at Delia and met her eye. He raised his eyebrows. She smiled and shrugged. He nodded. She spoke more to him than to the inspector. 'Any two siblings with very similar temperaments,' she said, 'are bound to disagree from time to time, and of course they know exactly how to hurt. Our childhoods were punctuated by hissing, screaming fights. I was the younger, so the fault was usually mine. But we got on much better in recent years, after we grew up. Far as I can remember, I don't think we'd had an argument stronger than a reasonable discussion in the last eight or ten years.'

'And is it not true that you were taught at school how to fall and roll.'

'You don't have to answer that,' Julian said. 'Almost everyone learned at school how to vault over the high horse and roll on landing.'

'I wasn't,' said the inspector.

'Then you must have grown up in a deprived area.'

The inspector glared but decided not to embark on a debate on the subject. 'And is it not true that your brother's death seems likely to treble your personal fortune?' he asked.

Julian was about to object but Delia spoke before he could decide on the grounds for his objection. 'I have no need of his money,' she said. 'I shall be quite well fixed with my share of the sale of the farm. And I'm not afraid of work, either.'

'That's quite enough,' Julian said. 'Miss Barrow is not going to answer any more of these questions which are clearly prejudicial, slanted and intended to provoke her into showing herself in a bad light.'

'I expected so,' agreed the inspector. 'Then perhaps it's my turn to provide information. It came to our attention that an application has been made for a replacement passport in Miss Barrow's name. I rather think that it may be some weeks before that passport is issued.'

'Now just a minute,' Julian began. 'Only the courts have authority to interfere with the issue of a passport to a British citizen. We need Miss Barrow's passport as part of the process of proving her identity.'

'No doubt the passport will be issued in time to prove her identity if any charges should arise from the death of Mr Barrow.' The inspector leaned forward to add empha-

167

sis to his words. His height, even seated, made the emphasis all the greater. 'In the meantime, if Miss Barrow's old passport should happen to make a miraculous reappearance, she would be very ill-advised to make use of it.'

Julian saw the two officers out of the front door. The inspector was thoughtful but brooding. Julian returned and met Delia's eye.

'Do they really think I killed my brother?' she asked. She did not look particularly surprised. Nor, on the other hand, did she look anxious.

He lowered himself into the chair vacated by the sergeant. 'What they think has little to do with it. It wouldn't matter if the inspector still believed in Santa Claus. The question is whether they can make a case.'

'And can they?'

'They might. It depends on what witnesses they can turn up. Evidence can get a little twisted when a witness thinks that he knows what the police want him to say. Tell me about the fatal accident in New Zealand.'

She met the question head-on. 'It was about four years ago. One of the hands was driving into town in a Japanese four-by-four

168

with a trailer and I decided to go along to do some shopping.'

'He was driving?'

'Yes. He wasn't that great a driver but he had wandering hands and I'd smacked his face for him only a few weeks earlier. You're safer from that kind of thing if you're a passenger. Coming back, the trailer was laden. On a steep downhill I could feel that he was losing it, so when he said "Jump!" I jumped. He couldn't make the next bend and he went off and over a steep drop into the river. Our police had a damn good look at the scene and the vehicle and decided that there was nothing wrong, so can that inspector get away with turning up here and throwing that sort of allegation around?'

Julian shared the last of the whisky between their two glasses. 'He hasn't stepped over the line yet. He was just probing for signs of a guilty conscience and you came through with flying colours.' He yawned and stretched. 'We'll just finish these drams and then I think we'd better get some sleep. We may have a busy few days ahead of us.'

Eleven

In the morning, Julian was up and breakfasted before Delia had stirred. When she made an appearance, tousled and looking very young, he was granted a moment of insight. He had never concerned himself much with matters of sensuality, being more concerned with life and the law. When others had referred to an appearance as being 'sexy', he had not really taken in the true meaning. But now there was about her the look of a pretty girl just jumped out of bed and ready to return to it. It seemed almost intrusive to look at her at all and yet impossible to wrench his eyes away. His hormones stirred in their sleep.

He noticed that among her purchases she had included a dressing gown. If it had been intended to lend modesty to her inevitable appearances in pyjamas, he thought, it missed the mark. It was knee-length, to be sure, and loose-fitting; but it was thin and silky and where it made contact with her person through her equally thin pyjamas there was a highlight rippling over the surface of the cloth that showed off each seductive, feminine curve. Was she as unaware of her sexuality as she seemed, he wondered? Indeed, was she capable of envisaging the effect that such a cloth would have on her figure, and on the male viewer? Or were girls born with an instinctive understanding of what will enhance their sex appeal?

His protective instinct was also roused by the fact that Delia was worried. 'I can't help wondering what they think I've done,' she said over breakfast. 'What are we going to do?'

'Nothing precipitate,' Julian said. 'We might make bad worse. They must be imagining you setting up the accident and then hurling yourself out of the car. They may be able to think along those lines but I can't see them convincing a jury that you would take such a physical risk. Not unless they can produce a witness or some forensic evidence, which seems highly unlikely. I know I said that we were going to have to rush around a bit but the time isn't ripe. We'll have to wait and see what kind of muck Mr Maclure starts slinging. Just relax for the moment and take it as it comes.'

It was not easy advice to follow but she did her best. Despite the problems posed by her injuries, she managed to shower and to take the time to turn herself out tidily in a new summer dress, delicately perfumed and with her hair in a pageboy; but Julian could not help hankering, just a little, for the earlier Delia, she of the thin dressing gown and hair like a gorse bush. She might have been more approachable than this model-girl, if he had had the nerve.

Next morning at least one period of suspense was over. A major Scottish tabloid carried the story of Aloysius Barrow's death and the police enquiries. It was not attributed to Mr Maclure but his byline might as well have been printed at the head of every column. Factually it came close to accuracy. Julian read it with great care. The size of Delia's probable inheritance was mentioned more than once. There was no open allegation that Delia had been responsible for the accident or the death, but it would have been an unusual reader who had not finished reading with that impression implanted in his mind. It was not actionable, it was merely sickening.

As Julian was to discover, Delia – or Dell as she insisted that he call her – was almost the perfect guest. She never asked to borrow his car but occasionally she would take the bus or beg a lift in order to do a little shopping in Dornoch or Tain or Bonar Bridge. Generally she was around, inconspicuous even when she was at her most helpful. The damage to her left arm had turned out to be a severe sprain to the wrist with no broken bone. Her left leg had been damaged to the extent of a greenstick fracture to the fibula. She was walking, albeit with a stick, but she helped Geordie to finish the proper spare room and almost single-handedly moved herself and the furniture back into it. As May Largs's design for the garden matured on paper, she was invited to sit in on discussions in which her comments were constructive and to the point although she was disadvantaged by her unfamiliarity with the Scottish climate and native species. Grace was using her physio-therapeutic skills to restore muscles that had softened during the period

173

of bed-rest and the continuation of limited activity. The two made plans to run together when Delia's leg was fully mended.

Delia took over the cooking, producing some unusual but delicious dishes from ingredients already in his cupboards or freezer. Julian and Grace encouraged her to use her left hand. On her third evening, she produced lamb chops. 'You bought these?' he asked her.

Dell seemed to flinch. 'Only off the van. Is something wrong with them?'

'They're delicious.' He put down his knife and fork and looked at her. 'Perhaps I should have warned you, but I thought that there was plenty in the big freezer. I have my own foibles about what I eat.'

She returned his look anxiously. 'Well, you're not always vegetarian. I noticed that much. You took a vegetarian dish when we lunched out on the way here, but you've been eating meat since then. There's plenty of venison in your freezer, salmon and trout, pheasant and pigeon breasts but I thought that you could do with a change of flavours.' She sounded almost tearful.

'Very observant of you.' He gave her a look that was both solemn and shy. 'You may think I'm mad but it's time that I explained my philosophy, such as it is.'

Dell took comfort from the fact that he was eating his lamb chop. 'Go ahead,' she said.

Julian nodded. 'I think vegetarians have the wrong end of the stick, if they think they're doing the animals a favour. If we were all vegetarian, most of the land – at least the land with water available – would be needed for vegetable crops. All the domestic and most of the wild animals would virtually die out. So I see nothing wrong with eating meat. When I eat out, I may not be given much of a choice, but I do have a conviction that anybody eating meat or fish but relying on other people to kill and prepare it for them is a damned hypocrite.'

'That's most people,' Delia said.

'I'm afraid so. But most of those who eat meat turn their minds away from what happened to the meat before it reached their table and they look disapprovingly on anyone who gathers his own meat. If a hostess puts down meat in front of me, I'll be polite and eat it – even if it's veal, of which I profoundly disapprove. At home, if I eat meat or bird or fish it's something that had its turn in the wild and that I caught or shot myself. If you want to laugh at me, go ahead. And if you don't enjoy a diet that tends towards trout, venison and pheasant, and even curried rabbit now and again, well tough luck!'

She was dumbstruck for a few seconds. He waited for incomprehension, ridicule or counter-arguments. 'How about that, then?' she said at last. 'That's a hell of a point to make to a one-time sheep-farmer. It's an upside-down way of thinking but I'm damned if I don't see a whole lot of sense in it. I always did feel a bit sorry for the sheep. Some of them became quite individual to me. Next time we fancy a bit of lamb, I'll buy one that's still running around.'

He laughed but shook his head. 'There's no need to go overboard,' he said. 'We can't all hunt our own meat. The salmon aren't running yet, but when your wrist's a little stronger do you fancy coming with me to try for a few trout? There's the mouth of a stream near here where the trout seem to linger.'

'I used to cast a mean line. New Zealand's rich in fish.'

'I have permission to stalk any inferior beasts on two local estates, in return for keeping the estate on the right lines in dealing with any poachers. Do you like venison?'

She was laughing at him. 'I bet I've shot more deer than you have,' she said. 'And – what do you call it here? – and gralloched them. And filleted more fish. Like I said, we have plenty of those in New Zealand and not a lot of shops where I come from.'

'When the season comes round again ... But will you still be here?' he asked anxiously.

'I shan't be far away.'

Julian went about for the next hour with his lips pursed and his eyebrows up.

Part of the refurbishment was directed to the main bathroom, where the previous occupants had managed to install quite the ugliest tiles ever manufactured and to match them with the least suitable wallpaper. Julian and Geordie were planning to replace the whole suite and had begun by taking out the original fittings. With the only bathroom still in working order *en suite* with the spare bedroom there were inevitably occasions when he was granted an accidental glimpse of her in a total or partial state of undress. On one such occasion he began to apologize. She laughed, which he took as a sign that growing up in the masculine atmosphere of a sheep station had taught her not to over-react to an invasion of her modesty. 'Forget it,' she said. 'I'm not much to look at.'

'Rubbish!' Julian said, without pausing to consider his words. 'You have a beautiful figure. It's too good to hide away. You should show it off more.'

She blushed for the first time and seemed ready to fall over her feet. 'There isn't any more,' she said. By then, she had wrapped herself in a big bath towel but she could not expunge herself from his memory. Julian had been enchanted to discover, as best he could judge from the briefest of glimpses, that she had quite the most beautiful bottom in the world. He had suspected it from the high-lights flowing over that dressing gown, but now he could be sure. He just managed to stop himself from saying so. It was not yet the moment, or so he thought.

The week passed peacefully. Julian's efforts on Dell's behalf moved towards fulfilment. Her own bank account was transferred to Inverness and suddenly she was in funds, but on Julian's advice they put off making any moves towards proving her brother's will. A hint had reached him through Constable Weigh that the procurator fiscal was only waiting for some such evidence of a desire to inherit before calling for the enquiry before the sheriff that stands in place of an inquest in Scotland.

Sometimes Julian could spare time to help with the redecoration. With two and a half people giving it attention the work accelerated. By late in the following week, Julian was planning a trip to purchase the remaining paint and paper and to choose a colour for the bathroom fittings. He and Delia were about to enter his car when PC Weigh arrived suddenly, demanding a conference with Julian.

'You'll have to go,' Julian told Delia. 'Geordie can drive you – my car's insured for any qualified driver.'

'Gee! You trust me to choose all those colours?'

'Yes, of course. Your taste is more reliable than mine. And work resumes soon at the Canmore House Hotel, so we'll be losing Geordie.'

Dell turned pink with pleasure and hopped into the car. Julian led the PC into the sitting room, which was looking larger and emptier than before. 'I've got my study back,' Julian explained. 'Now, what can I do for you?'

'Let us rather consider what I can't do for you.'

Julian's mood did a nosedive. Everything had been going so almost well. 'You can't save my client from the wrath of your chiefs?'

Weigh shook his head impatiently. 'No, it's not that. Quite the reverse, in a way. They believe that there may have been some tin but that Mr McTaggart is exaggerating the quantity and value for the sake of his insurance claim. They feel that there is no evidence, but only grasping at a supposition, that the theft of the piping is connected with skid-marks in the road where Mr Barrow was killed. Skid-marks that might have been there for a week, for all that anyone noticed. I have just come past the place and you can see them still.'

'Does the landscaping firm agree that Dean Murray had a bandaged head?'

'They agree that he had a knock on the head but nobody saw him with the full bandage on. His parents deny that he ever had a bandage. It seems probable that they now realize that the young man was up to mischief and they want to save him if they can.'

Julian had been sure that the slowly grinding mastication of the law would eventually cough up the truth. It now seemed that his confidence had been misplaced. Unfortunately he had been placating Delia Barrow with assurances that if the law did not exonerate her and exact retribution for her brother's death a civil suit might have the same effect. That prospect of a successful libel action seemed to be receding.

'Do they really believe that Delia Barrow killed her brother?' he asked. 'That she jerked the steering wheel and jumped out, expecting him to be killed?'

The constable made a gesture of frustration. 'Nobody tells me a thing,' he said, 'but I have heard it suggested that the young man had been knocked out, or even killed, with some blunt instrument and that the car had been rigged to catch fire as soon as it crashed. Neither needs a great deal of ingenuity nor leaves much evidence behind.'

'But the car took a leap over the kerb and was still moving fast when it hit the wall. Getting out without being killed would demand both ingenuity and courage.'

'The young lady does not seem to be short of either.'

For a moment it sounded unpleasantly possible. Any evidence that had not been destroyed by the fire would by now have been destroyed by the weather or by the local authority's mower. Julian experienced again the doubts that he had felt about Delia on the first day. But no. The theory might have been conceivable if applied to some greedy, calculating, hard-faced adventuress; but applied to the girl he was coming to know, it was absurd. And he was talking to the wrong man. 'So where is Dean Murray now?' he asked. 'And did Fergus Donelly have anything to say?'

Weigh spread his lower lip in a moue, again clearly expressing frustration. 'Dean Murray has not turned up at his job at all this week. His parents believe, or pretend to believe, that he has gone to stay with his auntie in Granton, but his aunt has seen no sign of him. Or that's what she says.'

'In other words, you are getting the run-around.'

'That is so. Fergus Donelly, now. He lives between Inverness and Beauly, but his work brings him up here when he works. He seems to be mostly self-employed and he has not been taking on any work lately. I am told that he has a bad reputation. Murray's reputation is for mischief only, but Donelly's is serious. One or two minor convictions. Prosecution for a more serious offence of breaking into a warehouse but the only witness failed to come up to scratch. We think that he was threatened. Donelly has been involved in fights when it was uncertain who started it but there is little doubt who came out on top. A typical story, you might say, of a vicious young man skirting the fringes of crime and getting away with it for the moment. One of these days...'

'One of these days,' Julian finished for him, 'he will find that he has gone too far to turn back.'

'Just so.'

'Any other regular associates?'

Weigh shrugged. 'You could find all this just by asking around, so I may as well save you the trouble. There is a friend of Donelly's, named Cadiss – with two s's,' Weigh added as though that made it worse. 'Where do they get these outlandish names from?'

'Probably from Spain,' Julian said. 'I expect that it was originally Cadiz, brought in by a survivor from one of the Armada ships wrecked along this coast. From the way you said the name, I gather that he's a tough nut.'

'Yes indeed. To much the same degree as young Murray except that he is not so slippery and he has done time for assault and threatening witnesses. He sleeps in a caravan on a farm near Muir of Ord, but he rents a bit of grazing and keeps a few sheep near Cairnfauld. But this you may find interesting. When he works it is as a plumber and he did some work at the Canmore House Hotel. It is still a remote connection.'

Julian wondered whether it was worth bothering to argue with a traffic constable and decided that it could be. 'But it is a connection all the same,' he said forcefully. 'We have somebody with a criminal record and who was very likely to spot that the hotel plumbing was mostly in solid tin, worth about eight times as much as the same weight of lead. He is associated with two other men of questionable reputation. The hotel piping disappears and an overloaded van forces a car off the road, with fatal results. The van was driven by a man with a bandage on his head, which at that time fitted one of the associates.'

PC Weigh was shaking his head slowly and sadly. 'But all that you say may be true or it may not. In the eyes of the authorities much of it is only according to a young lady who, even if she is truthful, was only half a second away from an accident and then suffered serious concussion,' Weigh pointed out. 'I am only looking at it through the eyes of my superiors, you understand? Anyway, not one of the three has been seen around here since then and my chiefs are happy to have it stay that way. We're understaffed and busy. We've had an outbreak of rioting at a football match, too many examples of seriously dangerous driving and four fatal accidents on the A9. We can well do without spending more and more time investigating a fatality for which the procurator fiscal already has a satisfactory explanation.'

'Then why is precious time being wasted on it?'

'Nobody is quite prepared to close the file. It is a loose end and the system does not tolerate loose ends. For your part, why are you so interested in the fatal accident? Is it the possibility that your client might be charged with murdering her brother that is concerning you?'

'I don't accept that there is any such possibility. But if we can prove that the brother was forced off the road by another driver, any other accusation falls to the ground and several files can be closed.' In his mind, Julian ran over the available facts. He seemed to be wading through a morass of cross-purposes with no firm ground at all. What emerged was another question. 'Has anybody checked along the side-road past Craigieshaw, where the van seems to have come out? Is there any sign of smelting having gone on?'

PC Weigh looked more uncomfortable. 'There is and there isn't. There's a tumbledown and roofless byre with signs of a fire, where Cairnfauld used to be.'

'Cairnfauld?' Julian said sharply. 'Where Cadiss runs his sheep?'

'That is so. They have recovered a whole load of firebricks that had been stolen off a building site. Just what shape they had been built into, we don't know; but there are ashes from wood and coal.'

'And that didn't start them thinking?'

Weigh was definitely avoiding his eye. 'It started them thinking about somebody living rough. It is not a place where smoke or firelight would be seen. Forensic has been asked to look for traces of smelting.'

Earlier, Julian had accepted Weigh as a young but competent officer who would do his twenty years without distinction and then move into security or body-guarding. But from the defensive tone of the other's words he recognized an inner man who really cared about his work and the relationship between police and public. He had a momentary vision of PC Weigh progressing up the ranks.

He made up his mind. 'It seems that the police are looking into the theft of the piping and into the fatal accident, but they do not intend to look very hard for any connection between them.' He waited to observe the constable's reaction.

Weigh shook his head. 'You can look at it like that, if you wish. But I have been told that I may look further into it provided that I do not neglect my traffic duties.'

'I, on the other hand,' Julian said, 'have two clients, each of whom would be very much interested to know the answer. That entitles me to ask questions of my own.'

'I can't argue with that. I will help you if I can.'

*   *   *

PC Weigh accepted his customary dram of malt whisky without any quibbling about going off duty. When he had sped the officer on his way, Julian sat down at his desk with the Yellow Pages. Dell came in at last, eager to tell him about the choices she had made.

It took Julian very few minutes to see and approve, quite sincerely, Dell's choices of colours. She had a very good eye indeed. Then he explained his discussion with PC Weigh.

'Surely,' Dell said, 'you can't go around investigating cases that the police have in hand?'

'I can if I have clients who are affected and if the police don't want to know. Do you want to help?'

'Yes, of course I do.'

'I may need you to help me work through the list of scrap metal dealers. We want to know who has bought or been offered scrap tin recently.'

Dell was looking worried. 'Won't the police already have asked that question?'

'Probably. But do you think that the police will have got straight answers? Relations between the cops and scrap dealers are never very friendly.'

'You might have a point there,' Dell said.

'I know I have. But there may be a short cut.' He put down the Yellow Pages and then picked it up again.

Twelve

Delia rather expected Julian to rush at the new challenge like a terrier going after a rat, so she was surprised when he let several days pass while he worked with Geordie to finish the decoration and return the house to an orderly state. That was all right with Delia. Whatever he did, it would be the proper action and in her best interests. With her money at last available to her and the golf tournament now no more than a memory, there would have been nothing to hinder her from moving out, but neither of them suggested it; in fact the subject was avoided with care.

They took an evening off for pursuit of the

brown trout that gathered, so Julian said, at the mouth of the burn, waiting for insect food to be carried to their very mouths. It was a clouded, humid evening, perfect for the hatching of insects and the trout were in a greedy mood. A powerful insect repellent kept the midges away. Dell's left hand could at least control the run of the line and she could stand without discomfort, wearing a pair of Julian's waders, up to her waist in the water and supported by its buoyancy. With Julian's spare rod she could, as she had said, cast a mean line with her right hand, but she insisted on sticking to flies that she said would have done murder in New Zealand although the fish of Easter Ross seemed resistant to their charms. Julian, landing a succession of medium-weight fish, left her to find out for herself that ignoring local advice is not the best way to fill the bag.

On another evening, the first since the house had been returned to a habitable state, they sat down together. After two days of occasional drizzle and a cool breeze, the sunshine had returned and after an early dinner they had carried their drinks cautiously into the garden. Dell was becoming fiercely independent and managed, despite the need for a stick in her right hand, to carry her drink in her left with her almost mended wrist hooked through one of the unstable but otherwise comfortable folding chairs. The air was still except for the movement of birds but there were no midges. In the soft light the distant hills looked very close. To Delia, it felt almost indecent to have leisure to sit and enjoy the view and the scented air.

It was not to last. Julian disappeared into the house and came back looking pleased. 'This has timed itself rather well,' he said. 'I've just checked my emails. There was one from a former business contact in the scrap metal business.'

'A client?' Dell asked.

'Not quite. A witness in the case I spent the last two years on. A shipping arbitration.'

Delia was interested in any new light shining on the accident, but after so many upheavals in her life she had wrapped herself at last in the peaceful and stable existence at *Pog*. She needed a few moments to brace herself before emerging once more and facing up to the circumstances of her brother's accident. If it had not been for the possible threat to herself, she might have preferred to let that death fetch up among the myriad of unexplained deaths. As a further escape and for reasons of her own, she was also intrigued by the unexpected glimpse into Julian's professional life. 'What was the arbitration about?' she asked.

Julian, with half his mind still on the email, glanced to either side to be sure that they were a discreet distance from each hedge. One advantage of arbitration over court procedures is confidentiality. He answered absently. 'You probably remember the incident of the collision of two ships in the North Sea. One of them nearly made it to safety but went down in the mouth of the Peterhead Harbour of Refuge. The arbitration started out to settle who was at fault for the collision and I was engaged as legal clerk to the arbiter, but the whole thing grew and grew. When shipping gets delayed, the cost of the delayed cargoes, what they call "demurrage", escalates rapidly. There's a domino effect as all the neatly planned movements of cargoes have to be rescheduled. For months, all attempts to refloat the *Smosverik* – the sunken vessel – failed. There were ships that couldn't get out of the harbour, including a factory vessel, and trawlers had to carry their catches to other markets. More and more claims were added.

'And in the middle of it all, the appointed arbiter had a stroke and died shortly afterwards. I couldn't blame him, really. When I was appointed in his place I nearly had a stroke of my own, but I was the only person who knew the ins and outs of it and the whole case was becoming more one of legal arguments than of shipping technicalities, so it was the sensible move. And then, of course, some of the parties wanted to delay while others were desperate to wind it up. It was one enormous boorachie – a muddle, you know? – for two whole years, and with almost every party represented by counsel it was costing about as much as running the NHS.' He laughed suddenly. 'When it was finished I made it clear that I expected an hourly fee equivalent to that of the most senior of the various counsel appearing before me and to my surprise I got it without a quibble. That's how I can afford the improvements to this house and to take a break before going back to work as a solicitor.'

Dell heaved a deep sigh. 'I should bloody well think so,' she said. 'The judge should be paid more than the advocate. It's great to hear a story with a happy ending. At least, it was happy for you. I don't suppose all the – what would you call them? – the parties were as happy.' She braced herself for a return to the here-and-now. 'But you were going to tell me about your scrap merchant.'

'Yes, of course.' Julian paused to bring his mind back from a time when it had been preoccupied with maritime law. 'James Buchan wasn't a party to any of the disputes. One company tried to argue that there had been contributory negligence by sloppy maintenance of some radar gear that by then had already been recovered and sold to Buchan for scrap. So he had to be called to speak on the condition of the radar. He said that it was in perfect working order. It's still at work on one of the rig supply ships. I got to know Buchan later.

'Scrap dealers are always being offered stolen metals, machinery, components from stolen cars and the like. Their relationships with the police can get fractious, to put it mildly. A voice on the phone, asking about scrap tin just after the police had been asking much the same questions, would be unlikely to get an answer that didn't include the word "off". A trade enquiry by a colleague, even a rival, might have more chance. So I asked him to make some enquiries for us.'

'That was your "better idea"? I think it really was!' Dell commented. 'What did his email say?'

'He told me quite a lot about who not to bother with. Car demolishers, for instance, are always under the eyes of the police and wouldn't touch stolen bulk metal with the proverbial barge pole. Dealers in bulk non-ferrous metals are few and far between but he suggested the name of one who Derek McTaggart should contact for the sale of the sheet metal off his roofs. He phoned one or two who he knows, asking for suggestions as to where stolen tin might fetch up and each time the name of a dealer not far from Inverness was mentioned.'

Delia's eyes were large and round. 'So what do we do?' she asked. 'Go and see him?'

'That is the great big question. If he did indeed buy the tin, it could be stacked in his yard. Or it could be hidden away. Or, of course, he may already have re-sold it. If he still has it and knows that it was stolen, he may have melted it again and cast it into the shape of a flywheel, a Corinthian column or an erotic sculpture, possibly all three. I'm just thinking aloud,' he added.

Delia laughed. 'I thought that was what you were doing. Maybe we should let the police try their hands at it?'

'Perhaps,' said Julian. 'But the police don't seem predisposed to make the kind of effort that would lead to a sudden pounce and comb through the place, examining all his paperwork. Can you imagine a couple of beat bobbies told to go and check it out, visiting the yard and being shown several small mountains of scrap metal? "Help yourselves," says the boss. Well, they'd have no easy way to tell tin from lead, zinc or any other heavy, white metal unless somebody had given them an expert briefing, which somehow I don't see. What I *can* see is them yawning and farting, stumbling around the yard with unfocused eyes, stubbing their cigarettes out on the statue I mentioned just now, taking a few scrapings from any suitable-looking junk and going back to offer those samples for forensic analysis.'

Dell spluttered again with laughter. 'God! I can see those two cops. I think I'd know them if I met them in the street. OK. So what do we do? Go visiting?'

'Yes, I think that's exactly what we do. We'll

leave tomorrow morning and plan for being away for a night, just in case. In the meantime, dusk is near and flies will be hatching. Do you fancy another go at the trout?'

'How can I,' Dell demanded, 'when we're going away tomorrow morning, probably for the night? I have to choose things and pack.'

Julian looked at her in surprise. He never had a problem of that kind. 'Do you need help with your packing?' he asked.

'I don't have time to be helped.'

Julian nodded. He quite understood. Some labours may be speeded by an extra pair of hands, but only too often the old adage about too many cooks proves to be true.

Now that action was imminent, Julian was in a fever to get moving in any direction at all. It occurred to him that there was one avenue that he had left unexplored, leaving it to the police who might not go to any great trouble and were unlikely to tell him all about it if they did so. Grace was able to tell him where 'Cairnfauld used to be' and he decided to forego the fishing and instead, to save time in the morning, to combine a trip to the filling station on the main road with a visit to that site.

The filling station was on the point of closing, so he filled the tank first. When he went to pay, he asked the cashier, 'Do you get many pale or white vans here?'

She looked at him blankly. 'Dozens.'

'Have you seen Dean Murray driving one? You know him?'

The cashier was a lady in her thirties and quite possibly out of them again, but she showed a knowing smile. 'I know Dean,' she said.

'And have you –?'

'The police were asking the same. And I never saw him driving anything but his dad's Land Rover.'

'Do you know Fergus Donelly?'

Her face clouded. 'I know him too.'

'Have you seen him driving a white van?'

'He was in here about a week back but I don't know what he was driving. And I'm not going to talk about him so don't ask me anything else.'

'You're afraid of him?'

She looked at him blankly. Julian tipped her well. She might be more forthcoming, next time.

The light was going, dusk creeping across the land drawing peacefulness behind it.

Following Grace's directions, he found his way to where Cairnfauld had lain before changing farming practices forced its absorption into another farm. Against the still luminous sky and the reflected lights of Dornoch, what remained of the buildings stood out dark and gloomy. He left the car with its headlights cutting a path between the black shadows. He always carried a rechargeable lamp in the car. With its aid, he stepped over a fence and made his way among the tumbledown walls, tripping over fallen stones whenever he lifted the beam to look ahead. Once he tripped over a sheep – one of Caddiss's almost certainly – that fled indignantly into the darkness.

He found the roofless byre. It seemed totally uninformative. There was clinker and ash on the ground, soot on the walls and scraps of broken firebrick lying around, but for all he could tell they had been there for months. Conversely, although he knew very little about smelting, he could see that it might well have been used for the smelting of the tin. It would only have needed one fireproof container. A copper wash-boiler might be too easily melted. Perhaps a steel oil-drum with a temporary furnace built around it and a large ladle for transferring the molten tin to moulds of sand. But there were no signs remaining to interpret. If there had been any slag discarded he could not find it. The place could, as the constable had suggested, have been the temporary encampment of gypsies who, in their thrifty way, had taken away with them anything of possible future use. Probably anything of significance that the gypsies had overlooked had been removed by the police.

He turned to go but was stopped in his tracks as the beam of his lamp played across the one unblemished piece of wall. On the smoothly rendered surface was a lively drawing in charcoal. Over the caption, 'Are you sure that this is what they mean by "Helping the police with their enquiries"?' the artist had drawn a young woman undressing in the presence of two policemen, one looking shocked and the other delighted. It was a caricature, a comic exaggeration, but every salacious detail was perfectly depicted. The creator might never be an artist in the strictest sense of the term but there was no doubt of his talent with a line drawing nor of his (definitely not her) ribald sense of humour. The drawing leaped out as a live entity, rude and yet charming. There could be no doubt whose hand had drawn it and Julian suddenly understood how it came about that there had been so much ambivalence in the comments made to him about Dean Murray.

Julian was seldom further than a short walk from his car, so his camera usually remained locked in the glove compartment. The drawing was worth recording, if only as evidence that Dean Murray had spent time there. It formed another part of the chain of proof connecting the stolen tin with the death of Aloysius Barrow. But Delia, who had been familiarizing herself with its instruction book, had borrowed the digital camera only that afternoon for her own unspecified purpose. He slipped his cellphone out of his pocket and switched it on. Walking back towards the main road, he found and keyed in his own number.

A bright moon was showing a thin rind above the horizon but that seemed to make the shadows darker. There was no answer from *Pog*. But Dell had equipped herself with a mobile phone and he had programmed the number into his own phone. He found it and keyed.

The ringing tone was quickly interrupted

by Delia's voice. 'Hello?'

'Dell,' he said, 'do you still have my camera or did you put it back in the car?'

'It's right here. I have it in my bag.'

'Is the battery up?'

'I've charged it this morning.'

'I'm at Cairnfauld and there's something here that I think we should record. Get hold of Grace and beg her to bring you and the camera here. She knows the way. Failing Grace, get somebody else. Or phone for a taxi. It's important.'

'I'm already in a taxi. I was short of some odds and ends so I phoned for a taxi to take me into Dornoch and we're just coming over the bridge now.'

'That's good. I'll walk up to the main road and meet you.'

As he turned away, he almost collided with a large figure that had approached silently over the grass. He was in no doubt about the menace of the newcomer. Every movement suggested threat and the man's arm was poised as though holding a weight.

Julian had never been a fighter but he recalled that a friendly policeman, waiting in a witness room and discussing a recent spate of muggings, had offered some advice that seemed to be on the point of paying off. 'When all else fails, bring up your knee.' Julian tried it but found himself lacking in either accuracy or power. An instant later the night sky exploded into a multitude of coloured lights. He was only distantly aware of hitting the ground.

Thirteen

Delia paid off the taxi at the mouth of the Cairnfauld road. She had an uneasy feeling in her stomach. A white van had emerged from the side road and turned towards Inverness as they approached. She called out, but there was neither sight nor sound of Julian. Perhaps she had been precipitate in parting with the taxi. She hurried along the road and almost immediately the gleam of polished paintwork in the dying light revealed a car that turned out to have the familiar lines of Julian's. Fumbling inside, she found that the key was still in the steering column.

She called again, so loudly that it was almost a scream, but again there was no reply. That settled it. She sank into the car's driving seat. The layout and controls were almost identical to the car that she had shared with Aloysius and there was broad grass at the roadside. With a silent prayer that no ditch was lurking unseen in the gathering dusk, she turned the car and spurted back to the main road.

There was very little traffic. She had nothing to go on but hunch, and hunch was reminding her that a white van had already figured ominously in events. Julian had phoned her to meet him and he was not there. She could have stayed, fumbling in the dark to find Julian or his corpse, but hunch insisted that he was in the white van. She could not think of a single useful action that she could take except to stay in touch with the van and see what developed. From the junction she could see a long way ahead and the lights of the solitary vehicle approaching the bridge surely belonged to the white van. But there was one other step to be taken. She got out her mobile phone – what was the number for the emergency services in

Britain? Nine-nine-nine, she was sure that that was it. She keyed it in anyway, received an answer and advised the operator that a man might be lying injured at Cairnfauld.

She turned the car towards Inverness and floored the accelerator.

Julian drifted towards a surface, but he was aware of nothing but pain. It was not pain in any particular place, indeed it did not seem to be confined to his body but to be occupying the whole of space. Gradually, reluctantly, he drifted closer. He desperately wanted to be sick but he knew, by some intangible reasoning, that to do so would spell disaster. He tried again to locate the pain, but it was too widespread. His head hurt, and his feet, but not quite everything between.

He drifted away again, but when he came back he was clearer in what was left of his mind. He wondered what hurt the most, and why. His head was agony and, as he moved, it rubbed and bumped on a hard floor. But why was he moving? He had no wish to move again, ever. He tried to sleep but noise and movement kept him conscious.

Sickness came at him again but he now realized that his mouth was stuffed with some sort of cloth and there was another cloth round his face, preventing him from spitting it out. That was why he must not give way to sickness – he would be in danger of drowning in his own vomit. He tried to bring up his hand to pull it away but his hands would not move. It came to him that his wrists were tied together behind his back. His ankles also were tied and he was lying on the floor of a moving vehicle.

The whys and wherefores seemed, for the moment, to be of less importance than endurance and survival. He concentrated on fighting off his nausea.

Delia could see the roundabout from the middle of the bridge and the van seemed to go left, away from *Pog* and towards Inverness. When she reached the roundabout the van was already away round the curve. She followed as fast as the gears and the slope would allow. She hoped that it was all a false alarm, that Julian had retreated into the gloom to answer a call of nature, even if that meant that she was burning his fuel and thrashing his car unnecessarily. She passed the junction for Tain, but by then she could see a vehicle ahead that had to be the van.

She reduced the gap until she could see that it was indeed a pale van and she realized that she had been holding her breath. But was it the same van? And was Julian in it? She gripped the wheel and told herself that she would make an even bigger idiot of herself if Julian was indeed in the van and under duress and she gave up the chase. If something happened to Julian that she could have prevented she would never forgive herself.

There was a little more traffic now. Oncoming vehicles must be making it less likely that the van's driver would notice that he was being followed. All the same, she was relieved when two cars came out of a side-road and slotted themselves between her and the van. She let her lights remain dipped as if out of courtesy. The moon was well up, throwing black shadows but gleaming off the road. She could have reduced to sidelights and still seen the road, but that, she felt, might have sent the wrong signals to the other driver.

She had returned her mobile phone to her bag on the seat beside her. Even in the low and changing light she could surely switch it on and key in nine-nine-nine again. But what could she tell the police? 'I think that my solicitor has been carried off by one or more criminals in a white van and I'm following it south on the A-nine. My address? Well, actually I'm living in his house just now. And why do I think he's in trouble? He phoned me to meet him and then he wasn't where he said he would be and I saw a white van driving off and we think it was a white van that ran us off the road and killed my brother, days ago now. And ... and...'

And while she was being pulled over to explain to the police, the van would turn off and be gone. She had never even been close enough to read the registration number.

A faster car arrived from behind and joined the convoy just behind the white van, but the van was taking more than its fair share of the road and the car seemed to settle behind it. The van was coming up behind other traffic. It was becoming more difficult to pick out the van's lights among the others. Eye strain was beginning to tell. At any moment she might see a vehicle turn off and be left unsure whether it had been her quarry. White-knuckled and daring, she pulled out and overtook two cars. Oncoming vehicles flashed at her but she had never been vulnerable to dazzle and by stretching her neck she could screen the headlamps from her eyes. She gave the other drivers a signal with the fingers of her right hand which, fortunately, they could never have seen in the darkness. A car refused to slow to let her in. The driver must have thought that she would go further up the column of vehicles. She made a determined move and the other car gave way at the last moment with an angry flash of lights. She could feel the emanations of his resentment on the back of her neck. Now there was only one car between her and the van.

The van was signalling left, she could see the light reflected in the road surface. It was surely intended as an invitation to overtake. If she stayed on the van's tail she would become suspect but if she overtook she could lose her quarry. Could fate be so cruel? But the van was also slowing and there were signs and road markings for a junction. She dropped back as far as she dared.

The van turned off. She had to follow, but there was another and minor road to the left again, leading to a village. She took it, stopped, turned in a driveway and came back. The van was far enough off now and the moon was bright enough for her to run on the minor country road without lights. There were no other vehicles around but God protect her from a policeman on a bicycle. Nobody had told her that policemen in Britain no longer ride bicycles.

The road shaved past a large barn and the van turned off into what seemed to be preparations for a small housing estate.

'You're awake, are you?' said the driver. There was just enough light for Julian to see that there was no other passenger in the van. 'You bugger, you've caused us enough grief. If you'd had the sense to let it go as a traffic accident ... But no. You had to sniff around like a dog after a turd, and get the filth looking for one of us. Well, that's more than enough. You're going to disappear. If we can fix it, the girl will vanish too. They'll draw the obvious conclusion. They may wonder for a while what the two of you were running away from but they'll forget.'

The van swung into the building site, bumping over a change in level and rolling Julian agonizingly across the van's floor.

Fourteen

Dell was confused. The van had stopped in the middle of what seemed, from the pattern of shadows, to be groundwork for a small development of roads and houses. Was this the moment to howl for the cops? There could be a hundred reasons for a van to visit a building site after dark and a call to the police about such an innocent visit might invite questions that Julian would have preferred to leave unasked. She decided to take a look. She left Julian's car in the shadow of the barn and set off on foot, following the outline of a roadway but trying not to stumble on the uneven hardcore. She needed the support and steadying of her stick, but the stick made it more difficult to move in silence.

The van had stopped close to a large dig-ging machine – rather a large digger for a small site, but a builder may use whatever machinery he has to hand. The driver of the van had jumped out and was climbing into the open-sided cab of the digger. As Delia drew near, the digger's lights came on and the heavy diesel began to tick over. Delia took a step to the side into the shelter of what seemed to be a wooden site office.

The digger was set to work. The broad blade pushed back the hardcore over an area the size of a billiard table. Then it took a deep bite out of the ground beneath, swivelled on its tracks and deposited the load on an adjacent spoil heap. Returning to its first position it took another deep bite out of the earth, drawing back and waiting, ticking over quietly like an obedient animal at rest.

The driver returned to the van and backed up a few yards so that the van's rear doors were above the fresh excavation. Dell approached closer – the driver would not see her from his pool of light. Above the digger's tickover she heard sounds from inside the van. Then the back doors opened and a figure was pushed out, to fall heavily into the bottom of the excavation. The instant that she had it in view before it vanished into shadow was not long enough to allow her to make out any features let alone details, but Dell was sure that the figure was Julian's and that he was tied hand and foot.

Or was her imagination running away with her? Her heart was thumping, which told her very little. The intuitive certainty that had carried her along so far had petered out.

The driver stepped down and walked round the excavation, looking down on the figure below. 'Well, friend,' he said, 'this seems to be it. When I backfill the hole and smooth over the hardcore, nobody will suspect a thing. But you may not be alone for long. If we can grab the girl tomorrow you may find her in bed with you.' He laughed shortly. 'It's not all your own fault. If that daft bugger Dean hadn't run her brother off the road, none of this need have happened.'

That was all the confirmation that Dell needed. The driver continued rambling on similar lines. Dell took it that he was hesitating before the ultimate crime. That possible evidence of compunction may have saved his life. But she had stopped listening.

Delia was now in no doubt that she must move fast to save Julian. But she would be no match for the driver who seemed to be a bulky man, moving as though confident of his strength. She needed a weapon. Her stick was too light – no more than a cane. Nothing else came to mind and hand. Nobody had left a convenient hammer or crowbar for her to stumble over. The building industry is notoriously casual about tidiness but this site was the exception. There was only one object, the very largest thing around. She would be taking a sledgehammer to crack a nut, but it would have to do, Back in New Zealand she had been taught to drive a digger. It had been a similar digger though not identical. She climbed into the cab.

Her first intention had been to use the bucket of the digger with its load of clay soil to drive the man into the ground like a tent peg. At the last moment she decided against killing. She sent up another silent prayer, this time that the levers would be in the same sequence as they had been at home. Holding her breath, she tried them.

The big machine moved forward, ponderously but quickly. The lip of the bucket caught the man behind the knees and he sat down on the heap of earth in the bucket. She changed hands. The digger stopped just short of the brink and the big bucket lifted, up and up, until she stopped it at its very highest stretch. From that height an athletic man might have jumped and rolled to safety, but an overweight man past his first youth who, it soon appeared, suffered from vertigo, could only dig his fingers into the soft clay, hoping that that tenuous grasp would suffice, and close his eyes against the view of the ground which, in the moonlight, seemed a very long way below.

During the previous hour Delia had become habituated to taking quick decisions and acting on them. Her mind did a quick survey of the situation. She had nothing on her with which to cut whatever was binding Julian. To carry him to the car would be beyond her strength and any attempt might well damage her injured leg beyond repair. Very well, the car must come to Julian. She jogged carefully to the car and drove back over the hardcore. In her bag she had nail scissors.

The excavation seemed very deep and black but she managed to make out the figure below and to scramble down without treading on it. By touch rather than sight she found her way to the cords on his wrists and ankles. With some difficulty she cut them and then, as an afterthought, removed the gag from his mouth. He rolled himself over and was mightily sick. The voice overhead formed an unhappy background to her labours but she ignored it.

This was not the end of her problems. For a man already suffering concussion, a tumble into an excavation had been the worst possible treatment. Julian was dazed and disoriented. Delia coaxed him into sitting and then, shakily, raised him more or less erect and leaning against the earth wall. Somehow, pushing and pulling and cursing and bullying, she managed to get him up the easiest slope and out on to the ground beside the car. Then, holding him, she took a rest. It needed only a little more effort to move him into the passenger seat, but exhaustion was very close and it was an effort that she was hard put to make. She managed it in the end and when she lowered the seat as far as it would go he seemed stable. She clipped his seat belt on anyway. She was sweating and her limbs were shaking.

Before she drove off, the plaintive cries coming from the man marooned overhead on the digger's bucket reminded her of a score to settle. She climbed again into its cab and turned the big machine aside. Then she set it in motion and jumped out quickly. The last that she saw of it, it was heading across country in the general direction of the Cromarty Firth, bearing aloft its terrified passenger.

She drove Julian's car back to the main road and set off for Inverness.

He was aware, but in a vague and detached way, of pain in his head but that was less by far than the pins and needles as blood returned to his feet and hands. He remembered lying with his head in something infinitely comfortable that he somehow knew to be Delia's lap, then of his face being wetted by what he guessed were tears. A sharp stone had been digging into his hip. Then he was being pulled about and lifted and half-carried and vomiting again on to earth. He remembered her telling him to stop apologizing. He closed his eyes and was happy to sleep, to pass out or perhaps even to die to escape his many miseries.

Then he was half sitting half lying in a car that smelled like his own. Her voice said that it was his own car so he could be sick in it if he wanted to. Somebody gentle was driving. Time seemed to flick away. He was being lifted on to a trolley. Lights were shone into his eyes. He was on a hard bed that moved but he slept. He dreamed that he was sliding on his back through a miniature tunnel.

A long time later, as it seemed, he became more aware of his surroundings. He was on another, wider bed but just as hard. He opened his eyes but the agony of daylight was such that he closed them again quickly. They closed silently to his relief. There was a pain in his wrists and ankles that almost rivalled the one in his head. He wanted to be sick again but he knew that the act of vomiting would have triggered a whole range of unpleasant sensations. He was in a mental vacuum, which was where he preferred to stay.

A voice invited him to wake up, but that was not part of his life-plan. Then somebody dragged up first one and then the other of his eyelids and once again a light was shone inside. Julian said 'Hoy!'

'Hoy yourself,' said the person who he now assumed to be a doctor. 'How do you feel?'

That at least was a question worth answering. 'Indescribably awful.'

'That's about par for the course. You can sleep some more.'

'What happened to me?'

'Either you walked into a tree-trunk or somebody crowned you with one. There were traces of bark around the lump on your head.'

He slept again. He was roused by an odour, a scent, a smell. He had usually remained quite unaware of Delia having any personal odour or wearing any scent at all and yet he knew that she was not far away. He must have registered her fragrance when he was lying with his head in her lap. She smelled of a blue flower but he could not put a name to it. He dragged his eyes open. Delia Barrow was sitting by the bedside, watching his face. She smiled slowly and, he thought, beautifully. Something was familiar about the proportions of the single room or the quality of the light or the air. He was in Raigmore Hospital.

'How are you?' she asked.

'You tell me,' he said. The words hurt his head.

Delia made an effort to speak unemotionally, conveying the facts. 'You've been through the scanner. They say no bones are broken. They're waiting to check you for concussion. How much do you remember?

219

Don't force yourself,' she added quickly. Clearly after her own experiences she considered herself to be expert.

'We were talking about going somewhere. And I went to look at...'

'Cairnfauld. You called me from there. You wanted your camera. There was something that you wanted to record.'

'Did I say that? I wonder what it was.' He raised a hand and gently felt his head. Under a padded bandage there was a very definite and tender lump that was of him but not belonging. 'That's right. Cairnfauld. I spoke to the woman at the filling station. That's the last I remember. Do you suppose I made a pass at her and she beaned me with a jack-handle?'

She shook her head reprovingly but with a smile. 'You can't be too badly damaged if you can still make jokes, even if they aren't very funny. You said that it was important but you didn't say why.'

His headache was fading and, to his surprise, most of his brain was functioning. 'Never mind why just now. I may remember some day and then I'll tell you. Go on about what happened.'

'I was already in a taxi. I wanted some

supplies – women's things – so I phoned the chemist and he said that he'd open up for me. I was in the taxi and not very far from you when I got your phone-call. I got out where the Cairnfauld road joins the main road but you weren't there and, stupidly, I let the taxi go. A white van came out of there just as we arrived and I was getting to have a thing about white vans. I shouted and you didn't answer. I could only make a wild guess that you'd been in the van.'

Julian tried to chuckle without stirring up his headache. 'It's a pity that you didn't put money on it. You'd have got a thousand to one on a long shot like that.'

'Well OK, but I'd have won my bet. I just couldn't think of anything else to do so I followed it in your car. The only alternative was to look for you and see if you were lying unconscious or...'

Her voice failed her.

'Or dead?'

'Well yes. But if I'd done that I'd have lost the van. So I phoned the emergency services and told the operator that I thought there might be a badly injured man at Cairnfauld and hurried to catch up the van. It stopped in a building site. I parked in the shadow of a barn and walked on. He dug a hole under the bottoming or whatever you call it and I heard him – whoever he was – telling you that he was going to bury you there. So I got into the cab of the digger...'

'You can drive one of those things?' Julian asked.

'Certainly I can. Most places, when there's heavy work to be done, the person with least strength works the machinery. Haven't you seen quite small children driving tractors on farms? So whenever the access road got washed out I was the one driving the digger. I scooped him up in the bucket and put him as high as it would go. It would have been a long jump down and he wasn't exactly athletic – and I don't think that he had a head for heights. Anyway, he just clung there sounding scared. So after I'd fished you out I sent him trundling away cross-country.'

'That was kind of ruthless.'

'It's the way I felt. I just wanted him well away from me.'

Julian laughed as gently as he could. 'You are without doubt,' he began. Then he fell suddenly and soundly asleep, leaving her to wonder what he thought she was. Irresponsible? Stupid? Weird? Beautiful? Ugly?

Fifteen

Twenty minutes later he woke up suddenly. 'A very clever girl,' he said. He seemed quite unaware that there had been any break in their conversation but his speech was more fluent. 'It's all a bit upside-down, the damsel galloping to the aid of the knight in distress. Have the police been told anything?'

'No. I wasn't sure what you'd want and I didn't fancy telling the story to a pair of disbelieving, hard-nosed cops.'

'You surely couldn't call our friend PC Weigh hard-nosed?'

'Well no. He's rather cute.'

'Now that he is not,' Julian said indignantly.

They were interrupted by the arrival of a nurse who looked much too young to be given any responsibility at all. 'You were only supposed to be here for a minute or two,' she told Delia. 'This patient isn't supposed to be excited.'

'I don't think I excite him much,' Delia said. She made it sound like a joke but inside her mind the words were sad. During her stay in his house, she had come to appreciate Julian's quiet humour, his intelligence and his help. His lack of interest in her as a female person she had appreciated rather less. She had grown up in male company but under the protection of her father and then her brother. Now that their protective smothering was removed she was ready to respond to the next man to give her help and lift her burdens. Once or twice, greatly daring, she had ensured that Julian would accidentally glimpse her in the nude or the minimum of underwear. Any one of the workers on the sheep station would have reacted, but he had been the perfect gentleman. This made her respect him more, but a perfect gentleman was not what her fancy desired. Someone more amorous would have been to her taste. Not quite a ravisher perhaps, but tending slightly in that direction. The strong and silent type. Masterful.

'I wasn't excited at all until she said that she thought the traffic cop was cute,' said

Julian.

The nurse stifled a giggle. 'Well, don't say it again,' she told Delia. She looked at Julian and winked. 'I think you do excite her. You should have seen her when –' Realizing that Delia was making faces at her, she broke off and left the room.

'How long have I been in here?' Julian asked.

'Not long. You were only whacked last night and they gave you something to make you sleep. It's still morning, just. They let me sit with you because apparently it helps the patient to hear a familiar voice. Only I ran out of things to say.'

Julian took note and filed away for future reference the fact that he had at last found a woman who ran out of things to say. Delia had fallen silent, so apparently she had done it again. Before he could think of a topic to fill the gap, the doctor returned with the same nurse in attendance. Delia was sent out of the room while Julian was examined again. He agreed that his headache was abating.

'Mild concussion,' said the doctor. 'You can go home tomorrow.'

'I can go home today,' Julian said.

'I can't keep you here against your will,' the doctor admitted. 'But I'd have to give you a letter telling you that you mustn't drive a car until this time tomorrow.'

'I'll accept it,' Julian said. 'My lady friend can drive me.'

With no more than slight nausea, Julian managed to eat the hospital lunch. He was left alone to dress himself. His clothes seemed to have picked up more dirt than he would have expected from lying on the ground, but it was dry dirt. The ward sister produced a clothes brush and Delia brushed him down. The authorities accepted no responsibility for his sense of balance, so he was wheel chaired down to the door where Dell was waiting with his car. It was almost exactly the converse of the day when he had brought her away from the same door.

'You realize that you're bloody mad?' she said.

'I know it. But there's no cure for what ails me except time and rest and I can have plenty of both and be as mad as I like at home.'

'Yes. And what they call TLC,' Dell said. She wondered whether he would pick up the

226

oblique reference to loving.

He must have slept because suddenly they were crossing the long, low bridge over the Cromarty Firth. His mind must have been working while he slept. 'Don't take the short cut over the hills,' he said. 'Go round by the main road. Take me to where you got out of the taxi.'

'I don't call that rest. You're still bloody mad.'

'It might bring my memory back.'

The traffic was nose to tail. It was another half-hour before they turned off the main road. Dell pulled up on a grassy verge. 'Can you walk?'

'We won't know until I try. May I lean on you? My sense of balance...'

'Do you think I don't know the feeling? Lean against me for balance but don't put any weight on me if you can help it.' There was a comfortingly heavy walking stick on the back seat. With that and an arm around Dell's shoulders, he managed to hobble over the uneven ground without putting any strain on her still tender leg. In bright daylight the idea of somebody attacking out of the dark was not to be entertained. And yet, fragments of memory swam like fish in a darkened pool. He could see the doorway of the byre, a good stone's throw away. 'I'm remembering bits and pieces,' he said.

'That's how it comes back.'

'It seems, from the state of my clothes, that I was dragged,' he said. 'That raises the interesting question as to why I was attacked at all. And then dragged. I can't see what anyone could have got out of it.' The thought in his mind was that it would have been easy to kill him while he was at the mercy of whoever had knocked him out. It might have been the wisest move on their part, though he had more sense than to say so. Of course the driver had been at risk of a breakdown, an accident or a confrontation with the police. Better to be caught with an abductee than with a corpse. 'Except...' he said. 'Let's look inside the byre.' They progressed as far as the door of the byre.

'Now, that's very interesting,' Julian said. 'I have a recollection of a drawing here. I can't remember what of, but it was funny, a jolly sort of cartoon, and it was cleverly executed. Just the sort of thing that we're told Dean Murray is good at. Somebody dragged me out of the way and then seems to have scrubbed over it with a slurry of ash, cement, charcoal and I don't know what else.'

Delia sniffed the wall. 'Manure,' she said.

Through their close, physical contact he could feel her overtaking his reasoning. It seemed that they were developing some sort of telepathic connection, or else he was learning to read her body language. 'There might just as well have been a sign reading "Dean was here",' she said, 'and somebody wasn't happy about it. That somebody may have come here to erase it and found you already looking at it. He was feeling guilty and vulnerable because the theft of the tin had led to a fatal accident. He may have heard you phoning for your camera. Yes? And the presence of the drawing here fixes Dean Murray on the spot where the tin was melted and so connects the tin-smelters with the death of my brother.'

'That's how it looks to me. And now –' Julian swayed and had to grab her shoulder, '– I think I should head for home and bed.'

'I think so too. We're a proper pair of cripples.'

'Yes. On the films,' he said, 'a man may be knocked unconscious one minute and return to consciousness ready to jump up and hurl himself into another fight. Well, I may say that my faith in the veracity of Hollywood was never strong and what there was of it has been severely dented.'

'But not your skull.'

'No, not my skull. That's suffering nothing worse than a tender bruise and a severe onset of stupidity.'

Delia fed him what she considered to be a suitably invalid diet. He slept dreamlessly and rose in the morning feeling much restored by sleep and aspirin. They listened to the morning news over breakfast. It was reported that a digging machine had been stolen from a building site near Invergordon and had been found overturned several miles away.

'Nobody killed or badly injured,' Dell said. Julian could not tell whether she was pleased or disappointed.

Julian intended to pursue their aborted trip, but Delia put her foot very firmly down. 'It takes longer than this to get your strength back after being knocked out,' she said, 'and I should know. Rest today and we'll think about it tomorrow.'

He agreed with reluctance, but in fact when he settled to dealing with the minutiae of restoring Dell's identity he found that he tired quickly. He was glad to be interrupted in the middle of working on his draft application to the High Court by the arrival of Dr Dawes. Raigmore, it seemed, had been concerned about his injury and refusal to be kept in bed, sufficiently so to notify the local practice. Dr Dawes shook his head and tutted, but those seemed to be spontaneous reflexes because he congratulated Julian on the thickness of his skull, replaced the bandage with an adhesive plaster and advised him to stay away from tree limbs and baseball bats for a while.

Julian's appetite had returned and he made a good lunch. The washing-up was nearly finished when PC Weigh's small panda car turned in at the gate. Julian walked out to meet him. 'You had better come in,' he said warily. 'Miss Barrow will be happy to see you. She thinks you're cute.'

'And I think that she is cute,' said the PC, 'but only in a brotherly way.' Julian nodded. That was the way that he would prefer the relationship to remain.

Delia was waiting in the sitting room with fresh coffee. She had taken one of the single wing chairs, so it seemed that however cute the PC might be he was not to share the settee with her. When they were seated, Julian said, 'What brings you here?'

'Can you not guess?'

Julian thought that he could guess but hoped that he was wrong. He shook his head. Delia, however, had no reservations. 'Raigmore phoned the cop shop,' she said.

'What ever became of medical confidentiality?' Julian demanded.

The constable shrugged. 'They would not have mentioned the state of your mind or your bowels,' he said, 'but when a patient comes in with signs of assault including the marks of ligatures on his wrists and ankles they are obliged to make a report. An Inverness officer went to interview you but you had already signed yourself out. Did you think that you could become involved in violence without letting us know?'

'I rather hoped that you would not need to know just yet,' Julian said. 'I have some useful theories that may solve problems for Miss Barrow and Mr McTaggart and possibly, though this is of lesser importance, for yourself, but I have as yet not a shred of proof. I had hoped to get some proof before telling all, but now that I think about it this might be a good time to put you in the picture.'

PC Weigh listened impassively, making notes while Julian and Delia each told part of the story. Only when they arrived at the sending of the man for a ride in the bucket of the digger did Delia depart from the strict truth, allowing it to appear that the digger's gear had been engaged by accident. Julian was surprised to realize what a fluent liar she could be.

When they had finished Weigh said, 'Let me see if I have this straight. You think that the stolen tin was melted down and cast into ingots in the shelter of what's left of the Cairnfauld cowshed. Dean Murray might have been there, though he has a full-time job so he would only be there at weekends and evenings at the most.'

'He was off work, injured at the time,' Julian pointed out.'

'So he was, so he was. It seems that he was the driver of the van, so it may only have been while he was waiting for the loading to finish that he drew a sketch on the wall. That might not have mattered, except that the grossly overloaded van oversteered and caused a fatal accident. That not only made matters more serious but the location of the accident drew attention to the road to Cairnfauld. Anybody investigating might well happen on the drawing, which was as good as a signature in a visitors' book. Suspicion of Dean Murray would draw suspicion on his associates, so when one of those associates came to scrub out the drawing or saw you taking an interest in it, he overreacted, knocked you out and hatched his own plan for disposing of you. Does that sum it up?'

'Absolutely,' Julian said. 'Except that you told me that Cadiss, one of Dean Murray's less respectable friends, rents a bit of grazing for sheep at or near Cairnfauld. So now that I've spilled all my beans, you spill yours. How far have the police got?'

Weigh told him that he had the nerve of the devil, but went so far as to say that a white van had been hired in Dingwall and had been returned there without damage. It had been hired in the name of a Mr Dooley and paid for in cash. 'There is no such address,' he added, 'as the one given by Mr Dooley.'

'And is there anything about the van to connect Mr Dooley with Dean Murray or any of his disreputable friends?'

PC Weigh shrugged. 'We don't know,' he said. 'I was already enquiring about white vans but there must be enough of them here-abouts to fill a multi-storey car park. I had word back this morning about a van that was returned to the Inverness firm yesterday morning, but by that time it was out on hire again to a man who's hawking dog coats and dog beds around the game fairs. His wife kicked him out because the coats and beds are the product of his fancy woman and we don't know who she is, so it may be some time before we get our hands on the van.'

'As usual,' said Julian, 'one step forward and two steps back.'

'Only two?' said Constable Weigh.

Delia had been showing signs of impa-tience. 'But what happens now?' she asked.

'Now,' said PC Weigh, 'you wait while I make a report. Somebody senior will have a word with you –'

'That would be Inspector Fauldhouse?' Julian suggested. (PC Weigh just stopped himself from saying that he was afraid so.) 'What we have to offer him is hypothesis with little to back it up. One good slab of evidence would give theory a push in the direction of fact. Pointing out to you where the stolen tin might be stored would surely give that push as well as validating Derek McTaggart's claim.'

The PC, usually so easy-going, was looking shocked. 'That is a matter that you must leave with the police.'

Julian was almost inclined to agree, but in Delia's view the PC's cuteness had suffered an eclipse. She had taken on board Julian's word picture of a pair of badly briefed constables prowling unenthusiastically through a scrapyard and stubbing out their cigarettes on whatever shape the tin now took. She repeated it almost verbatim but with great vehemence. 'I am not suggesting that you delay your report,' she finished, 'but at least don't treat it as urgent. Julian used his professional contacts to find out the most likely place for the tin to be. We could take a look from a distance, tomorrow, and let you know straight away if we see anything suspicious.'

PC Weigh pondered, frowning. 'Proper procedure,' he said at last, 'would require me to copy my report to CID. Common sense suggests that I send it through by email. But there are one or two supporting enquiries that I should make, such as speaking to your friend Mr McTaggart, and then I shall have to type it up. I think it unlikely that you will be troubled before tomorrow night. By that time, I shall expect you to have informed me of what, if anything, you have observed.'

From Delia's expression Julian gathered that the PC's cuteness was no longer in question.

Sixteen

Julian would have been happy to set off immediately, but Delia was convinced that he was not ready for such action. Julian did not explain that his impatience was caused by the knowledge that his attacker knew where he lived. Although nobody could suppose that another attack on him would limit the spread of damaging evidence, many attacks, some of them fatal, had been committed for no better reason than mere spite. However, Bonzo was the most effective intruder alarm that Julian could think of and so he borrowed the big dog from Grace.

Bonzo, who was quite contented anywhere that there was food, settled happily in the kitchen. But there is no point in merely being warned. Julian also slept with his shotgun, loaded but open, on the locker beside his bed. With those precautions taken, he slept deeply again.

He awoke refreshed and almost fully recovered except for the still tender lump on his head. In the light of the new day, the presence of his shotgun and ammunition beside his bed seemed over melodramatic so he smuggled them into the gun-safe hidden behind the hall cupboard. Delia would have preferred that he take at least one extra day of convalescence, but he pointed out that time, in the form of Detective Inspector Fauldhouse, would soon be pressing and that he was probably safer from further attack while on the move than stationary in a house that was becoming generally known as his home.

'I suppose that's reasonable,' Dell said. 'Who do I phone to cancel the milk?'

'I'll do it. You get on with your packing.' While he gave the message to the local dairy his mind was still at work although not with its usual freedom. When the call was finished he went next door to return Bonzo to his rightful family. There was no sign of any strangers watching either house. He caught Grace leaving the house for her morning run and asked her, 'Do you by any chance have a photograph of Dean Murray?'

Grace paused in her playful greeting to Bonzo. 'I know somebody who would have. Jenny Welles. She is a photographer. She does a lot of freelance work and she's very methodical about indexing her negatives. Her husband's a police inspector in Inverness. Hang on, I'll give you her number.'

Julian returned to *Pog,* leaving a delighted Bonzo to accompany Grace on her morning run. Armed with a number and a code that he did not recognize, he was soon connected with a friendly, English-sounding voice. He used Grace's name as an introduction.

'Yes,' Mrs Welles said. 'I've certainly got young Dean's image on file. Give me a moment to fire up the computer.' There was a long pause broken by ruminative noises. 'I have him in the background of some digital pictures I could email to you,' she said at last, 'but I doubt if they'd enlarge much without losing definition. I have better shots of him at his cousin's wedding, but they're on film. I could print off a good enlargement and post it to you.'

Julian had no desire to put up with the delays and uncertainties of the postal service. He was about to ask for copies by both means when he recalled Grace's mention of Inverness and it occurred to him to ask, 'Whereabouts are you?'

'I live in Beauly.'

'I think that Beauly's on my route for this morning. Could I ask you to make me one enlargement of each of the shots you have, straight away? I could pick them up around midday if you'll be at home. You can charge me the going rate plus a premium for immediate service.'

The voice was definitely smiling. 'My standard rate will do very well, thank you and I'll be at home. I'll see you later, then.'

'Tell me how to get to your house.'

They were on the road by eleven and went by way of Dingwall through picturesque, hilly scenery that mingled the wild with the cultivated. They reached Jenny Welles's house soon after twelve. Jenny lived high on the hillside behind Beauly, in a large but neat bungalow with a superb view over the

Beauly River and most of the way to Inverness. The garden was exquisite, showing signs of May Largs's touch. Julian decided that Mrs Largs must have many imitators, or else she was either a famous and hard-working designer or an inspired promoter of her own work.

Julian was presented with three needle-sharp enlargements showing a cheery-looking, pug-nosed young man. He had been caught dancing, and again while raising a glass to the bride and finally seated at a table with a girl sprawled on his knee. In the last shot he was noticeably flushed with drink and there were several empty glasses in front of him. His left hand seemed to have disappeared but there was no sign that the girl resented whatever liberties might be being taken beneath the table. Julian had all that he wanted but they were not allowed to escape without snacking on a bowl of soup, crusty bread, fruit and an oatcake and cheese apiece.

Back on the road, they crossed the Beauly River just above the Firth and turned towards Inverness with the open countryside around the Firth to their left but the hills of The Aird rising on the right.

Businesses after the manner of scrap metal dealing sometimes germinate in the shadow of bigger businesses on which they batten. Some have grown by imperceptible stages until they occupy city sites and are too well established to evict. In general, however, the planning authorities are vigilant in watching for these undesirable neighbours and directing them on to otherwise worthless sites, well out of the way of more respectable citizens.

Metalsave was an example of the last category. Several hectares of scrap metal lay heaped within a mesh fence in what seemed once to have been a small quarry dug into a wooded hillside. A row of inexpensive buildings formed one boundary and turned a corner. The yard was easily visible from the main road and lay only a minute's walk away. The yard and the road were connected by a broad, unsurfaced track that Julian thought must become a quagmire in winter. Space for parking had been allowed outside the fence although there was no other vehicle occupying it at the moment. Any cars belonging to the proprietor or his staff, if any, were indistinguishable from some of the wrecks that were dotted among the hillocks of twisted metal. The place looked deserted. Julian assumed that any manual staff had knocked off and gone home.

Julian parked close to the fence. 'It might be best if you waited in the car for the moment,' he suggested.

'I might take a rest. I was up kind of early.' Dell nearly finished by reminding Julian to be careful, but she remembered in time that such advice often provokes a man into acting rashly.

Julian walked through the gateway and between the piles of scrap. Some attempt had been made at orderliness. Cast iron was separated from rusting heaps of mild steel. Copper and aluminium had separate stacks of their own. A smaller pile of brass seemed to consist mainly of door furniture. Several of the vehicles in process of being dismantled had a corner to themselves. Beside them was a kennel, made from an old lorry cab, housing two guard dogs that watched him with evil eyes and lifted lips. He guessed that the fence was intended to keep the dogs inside rather than intruders out. They seemed to know better than to chase away customers during business hours.

A stout, balding man in oily dungarees

came out of a door and met him. 'How can I help you?' The accent was faintly Irish, the tone inviting without being friendly.

'I don't know that you can. I'm looking for something to make into a garden feature. I'll know it if I see it.'

The man shrugged. 'Look around. Call me if you see what you want.' He turned on his heel and went back into what Julian thought was the office.

Julian wandered round the alleyways between the piles of scrap. He was feeling rather foolish. He had taken trouble while he drove to polish his story, but he had failed to notice one huge snag. The place was full of large metal objects any one of which would make an excellent garden feature. An old harrow, a tractor wheel, the flywheel off a steam engine, those and other things would each set off a garden rather well. How could he escape without either buying at least one item or arousing the man's suspicions? He peered into and through the heaps of tangled ferrous metals. Potential garden features seemed to be in much more plentiful supply than ingots of solid tin.

Behind a partially demolished caravan, he stumbled across the whistle off some big

244

ship. The brass was tarnished but it would polish up. Suddenly he could see it as the focus of May Largs's design for his garden. He could even run steam out to it through a pipe from a calorifier fed from his central heating. He had a vision of waiting until one of his least favourite visitors was stooped admiringly over it before pulling on a very long cord ... He thought that he was becoming a little light-headed but there was an undoubted attraction in the idea of an unwanted visitor – and he could think of several who would qualify – being induced to bite his or her tongue or worse. Even a jump out of the skin might not be too much to hope for.

Reluctantly he let the image go. There was something sinister about the place. Perhaps it was the accumulated deaths of so many once valued artefacts. He turned to go and almost bumped into the stout man who had arrived silently behind him.

'See anything you fancy?'

'How much for the ship's whistle?' The man named a price that was stiff but not out of reach. 'I'll have to consult my garden designer,' Julian said and fled, almost taking to his heels.

Back in the car, Delia seemed to be dozing. Julian drove back to the road, trying not to hurry.

Without opening her eyes, Delia said, 'Did you spot it?'

'Not a sign of it. But the place gives me the willies. I think I made the boss suspicious.'

'I didn't even get out of the car,' Dell said, 'and I saw it. I even took a photograph.' Julian lifted his foot. 'Drive on,' Dell said. 'There was a small hotel we passed just along here. It's too early for dinner but we only had a light lunch. Perhaps they could do an afternoon tea.'

The small hotel appeared round the next bend, an attractive old building, half-covered with creeper, nestling against the hillside. The building was freshly painted and the gravel forecourt was tidy and free of weeds. Without a word, Julian parked the car and picked up the large envelope that Jenny Welles had given him. Delia took his digital camera out of the glove locker.

In a porch sheltering the main door of the hotel, a sculpture stood. It was about waist high. It was jocular and slightly amateurish in style. It showed an animal, possibly a goat, reared up against a rock. To that harmless scene had been added a few deft lines in chalk and charcoal. A smile – a definitely lubricious smile – transformed the rock into a squat animal. There could now be no doubt that the goat was having sex with that animal and that each was enjoying the act. It was humorous. It was clever. And it was inescapably rude. Delia was chuckling and Julian laughed aloud.

In the silent, panelled bar their footsteps seemed to ring. A plump, artificially blonde woman with a pointed nose was working on VAT returns behind the bar counter. She accepted their order of tea and scones and vanished into the hotel's hinterland.

As soon as she could be sure that the woman was out of earshot, Delia produced the camera and switched it on. She brought the last frame on to the little monitor. 'I don't know if you can see it, scaled down like this,' she said. They were alone but she lowered her voice anyway until Julian could barely make out her words.

'But that's me,' Julian said. 'Me and that man with the belly.'

'Of course. But look at the background. Those buildings have walls only half a brick thick and painted white. But just behind you and him, where there was once a double doorway for taking a vehicle inside, it's been closed up with larger, rougher bricks, built dry and then whitewashed to match the rest. It doesn't have the neatness that you get with proper bricks. To me, it looks just like I'd expect it to look if the tin had been cast into ingots, using sand moulds, and then built into a wall and whitewashed. What do you think?' she asked anxiously.

He studied the tiny image. The detail was too small to be sure of, but he was quite prepared to accept her assessment. 'I think you're brilliant. I'm going outside to telephone. If the tea comes before I'm back, make a start. Ask for strawberry jam to go with the scones.'

The time had arrived for calling on some senior and local help. Julian had entered Jenny Welles's number into his mobile phone in case he needed to ask for further directions. The quickest way to get a number for the Inverness HQ of the police was to phone Mrs Welles. He was soon speaking to Inspector Welles.

'The Super's out just now,' he was assured. The inspector's voice was deep and resonant and quite without any trace of Highland lilt. 'But I can reach him if it's important. I've been kept informed about your interest in the road traffic fatality and in the theft of the solid tin pipes.'

'I'm now in a position to show you where the tin ended up,' Julian said, hoping fervently that Delia's reasoning was beyond reproach. 'It's much nearer to Inverness than to Dornoch. And I can demonstrate the involvement of Dean Murray in the theft of the tin, which should go a long way towards confirming the connection between the two cases.'

'And your reason for calling me instead of Inspector Fauldhouse is...?'

Here we go, Julian thought. 'My reason is that I may have shown interest. You're nearby and I want the police to see and collect the evidence before it disappears again.' There was a silence on the line. Silences have an extraordinary capacity for conveying emotion and this one was expressing dissatisfaction. More was needed. It was time to play his last card, a dangerous one. 'Also, Inspector Fauldhouse has already made up his mind to a quite different explanation and I wanted to reach somebody whose mind was still open.'

Inspector Welles let that pass without comment. 'And what do you want from me?'

'I suggest that you join me.' Julian strained to read the faded signboard. 'I'm not far from Inverness, at the Balnagairn Inn. I would expect to show you the tin and at least an indication that Dean Murray had been nearby.'

Inspector Welles gave it some thought. Julian could hear him tapping the desk with what sounded like a pencil. 'I can get away in about half an hour,' he said at last. 'Allowing time for travel, I should be with you in less than an hour. And if this is a wild goose chase, I'll throw you to Inspector Fauld-house without the least compunction. As it is, I'm driving a coach and horses through the proper procedures.'

He hung up. Julian allowed himself only a momentary shiver before hurrying back into the hotel.

Seventeen

The blonde woman returned with a tray bearing a chromium-plated teapot, a plate of already buttered scones and a small dish of jam. It was raspberry jam but Della decided to accept it. Dell greeted the woman with a smile that she tried to keep reassuring and humble. 'My husband's just gone outside to use his phone,' she said. 'Won't you join me for a minute? I'd like to ask you something.'

The woman looked surprised but she lowered herself carefully into a chair. 'Just as long as it isn't for money.'

'It isn't for money.' Dell pulled one of the photographs of Dean Murray from Julian's envelope and pushed it across the table. 'Have you ever seen this young guy before?'

It was immediately evident that she had. Her face lost colour. 'He's been here.' She seemed about to jump to her feet, but then

251

she settled slowly back into the chair, still tense.

Dell smiled. 'He drew the face on your statue, didn't he? I recognize his style. I'm surprised you didn't clean it off. It's very rude.'

Despite herself the woman returned the smile. 'Why would we? You see much worse on the telly these days. People have been coming just to look at it and then they stay for a drink or a meal. Some think we don't know about it and they come in to tell us. And some want to complain. It's that good for business that if somebody washed it off we'd have to draw it on again. My man took photographs, just in case. There were two lads tried to lift the whole thing into the back of a van but my husband caught them at it and dusted their breeks for them.'

They seemed to be straying from the subject. Delia nudged the photograph of Dean Murray. 'Please,' she said. 'Tell me what happened when this man came here earlier. It really is important to me.'

The woman tensed up again. She hesitated, biting her lip. 'I don't know what to do,' she said at last. 'I can see that it might be important. I've been thinking maybe I should tell the police.' She looked sharply at Delia as she spoke. When there was no reaction to mention of the police she went on, 'He looked harmless but he was with two other men and they didn't look harmless at all. They looked hard. Not the kind of men to cross.' She looked at Delia for a moment and shivered. Then she lowered her eyes again to the photographs. 'One of them looked really evil. Unpitying. It's as if he didn't think of people as being real but as things, you know what I mean? I've been scared in case they came back.'

Her attitude was so intense that Delia was infected with the same awe. A shiver danced up her back and she felt hollow. 'Why would they come back?' she asked.

'If some things came out, they'd know that they could only have come from me.'

'Did they threaten you?' Delia asked.

'Not in words. That sort doesn't need to use words. I was really scared and a man like that always knows when he's put the fear of God up somebody. They can smell fear the way an animal does. But I suppose they're a long way off by now.'

'I'm dead sure of it,' Delia said, with a silent prayer that she was not inducing the woman to lay her head on the block. 'Go on. Tell me.'

Once the first words are out, it is easier to go on than to turn back. The woman seemed to be feeling relieved, little by little, of a great weight. 'It was about a week ago at this sort of time, the quiet time of the afternoon. I was looking out of the window, wondering when the evening trade would begin. A van pulled in.'

'A white van?'

'Not a bit of it,' said the woman. 'A small van, dark blue. The two men in it just sat waiting. They were the two hard-looking men I told you about. One of them kept looking at his watch. A little while later a larger van came in. *That* was the white one you were asking about.' She sounded as though she had conjured the white van up as a special favour to Delia. 'This man in the photograph got out and he nodded to the other two and then all three came in here. I served them drinks – the other two men took whisky and didn't care if it was the good stuff or not, but this one just had a half-pint. Then I left them to it and I went through to make myself a cup of tea.' She managed to chuckle. 'You can hear a lot from through there, more than you'd think. The bar used to be no wider than a passage but it was made bigger a few years back – not by much, but it meant taking down a thick stone wall and putting in a thinner, wooden one. Many a good laugh I've had, leaving a young couple in here but hearing what they said.'

'You're very naughty,' Dell said.

'For listening to them? They're the naughty ones, talking sex in a public bar. These ones seemed to be arguing about money. After football, it's what men most often argue about. I knew them by their voices. I heard the one with the hoarse voice say something about doing all the hard work. "You're only the bloody driver," he said. He was scary enough but the other one was worse; cold eyes and not a word wasted. She tapped the photograph. 'This one said, "Yes, but you made a balls of loading the van and now I can't go home, somebody's dead. I'll have to hide out." That's when I knew it was bad.'

Delia saw that Julian was re-entering the bar. She gave him a quick frown and a head-shake to suggest silence. He nodded and settled quietly at a different table, behind the blonde woman's back. 'Go on,' Delia said.

'Just after that there was a rap on the bar. I

went through and the one with the raspy voice paid for the drinks. They were all looking angry but this one,' she tapped the photograph again, 'he also looked scared and I could see his hand shaking. But he'd made up his mind, I could tell from the way his jaw was set and the look in his eye. He wasn't going to give in, none of them was. In this trade you get to read the signs, what they call body language, and I knew there was trouble coming. Any time I see men like that in the bar, I tell my man to get ready for a fight to break out. Usually he can handle things just with his hands and fists, but if there's too many or too rough I fetch out the old cricket bat I keep under the bar and give it him. But I'd have called the police long before that.

'They went out and sat in the blue van. If they had a fight off the premises we didn't have to concern ourselves. I got on with my work but I kept the cordless phone handy. A little later I heard a van drive off. I looked out and the white van was still there.

'Customers began to come in. That's when we get busy, when men working in Inverness start heading home and stop off for refreshment. Sometimes, when I passed a window,

256

I saw that the white van was still here. It must have been two hours later when the blue van came back. The two men came in, the rough ones, but I didn't see your laddie. The two men came into the bar and had a large whisky each. I noticed that their clothes, which hadn't been clean in the first place, were earthier than before. They were talking in whispers. Then one of them, the one with the hoarse voice, said, "I must have left it there," and the other one called him a name I wouldn't want to repeat and said, "Well, go and get it, then." "I don't want to go back there," said the first one. The other one looked at me to be sure that I wasn't listening but I was clattering with the bottles. "What you want has bugger-all to do with anything," he said. "You bloody go, because if I think you're going to attract the wrong sort of attention to me I'll put you along with that other so-and-so." That really put the fear of God into me, because I've been trying ever since to put some other meaning to the words and I can't. And I knew that if they were pulled in over what I was thinking they'd know fine that it had to have come from me. You won't drop me in it?'

'Things have moved on,' Delia said. 'They will come to a head soon and whatever comes to the notice of the police could have come from any one of a dozen other sources. What happened next?'

'I pray to God you're right,' the woman said with feeling. 'The first one drove off in the blue van. He was soon back and came to the door of the bar and gave his friend a nod and the two of them went off together, one in the blue van and the other driving the bigger, white one. That's the last I saw of them.'

The bar was so quiet that they heard the creak of a floorboard where the woman had stood earlier.

'I can see what you're thinking,' Delia said. 'But maybe you're making something out of nothing. This young man could have been picked up by some other friend. The fact that you didn't see him again doesn't mean a thing. He might have left his own car some-where nearby for collecting. All kinds of maybes.'

'That's so. I've been telling myself that, over and over, don't think that I haven't. I've not much to go on except their manner. First they were eager for something. Then they were angry. In the end it was a sort of satisfaction mixed with excitement, like a man sometimes is after sex. You know what I mean?'

Delia said that she did. At the same time she was trying to tell Julian, by means of a look and some suitably modest body language, that she had no idea what the woman was talking about.

'I think a man would be the same after doing something really, really bad,' the woman said.

The bar fell silent, but the woman had suggested that going-home drinkers were due and, sure enough, two cars pulled up in front of the inn. The woman was about to rise but Delia said quickly, 'One more question, but it's very important. How long was the man away for? Could you make a guess?'

The woman smiled. Now that she had unburdened herself she was fully relaxed as though she had laid the whole of the burden on somebody else. 'I can do better than guess,' she said. 'Some of the going-home drinkers, the single men, like a bowl of soup, just to keep them going until they get home and make themselves a fry-up. I looked at the clock as I put the soup on and I gave it twenty minutes. That's how long it takes and that's just how long he was gone.'

The blonde woman had nothing else new to tell them, but now that she had started talking she could hardly be induced to stop. They tore themselves away at last, promising to return. Back in Julian's car he took the passenger seat and said, 'I told you that you were brilliant but I was only guessing. Now I know it for sure. You drive back to the scrap-yard. Let's see how long it takes.' He looked at his watch.

While she drove, he used the redial facility. Inspector Welles, it seemed, was already on his way. Police HQ in Inverness was unable to connect Julian with the inspector's mobile phone but promised to relay the message that they would be at Metalsave.

Delia parked outside the wire. 'Four and a half minutes,' Julian said. 'Call it five each way. That leaves five minutes to get up the hill and collect whatever he'd left behind and five to come down. I think you'd better wait in the car again.' The woman's fear had infected Delia and the idea of being left in the car was less attractive, but she had to admit to herself that her leg was still far from the condition required for a climb up a hill against the clock. 'I suppose so,' she said.

'Fine. Lock yourself in; keep the engine running and if anything worries you just drive off. I'll look out for myself and we can phone each other.'

That seemed to Delia to be a reasonable programme. She took her phone out and switched it on. Julian did the same.

As Julian began climbing, the fat man in the office was picking up the telephone. 'He's here again,' he said.

There were several minor paths made by rabbits or deer but there was only one track of human scale leading up the hillside from behind the scrapyard. It began outside the wire fence where the old quarry wall was lowest and, because the place had been a quarry, the ground was rock. Faults in the rock created a stairway of sorts and he thought he could detect signs that human hands had rearranged a few large stones to improve the going. Julian pressed on and, as he climbed, he studied the ground while at the same time darting occasional glances at his watch.

Above the lip of the quarry, about level

with the roofs of the low buildings, lay a strip of bare ground, too hard for anything but scattered tufts of grass. Here the track became invisible, but soon the stony ground gave way to soil and almost immediately a plantation of young conifers began and the track resumed as a break in the trees. The trees had been planted ridge-and-furrow, so there must be another and better access for machinery. Here, a growth of weeds showed signs of the passage of feet but Julian knew that the tree roots would be too thick for grave digging. Anyway, the eventual harvesting of the timber, well within the lifetime of the criminals, would uncover a body and trigger the hue and cry. Any killer with sense would have gone higher, no matter what burden he was carrying.

Between the trees, the air was close, almost breathless. Midges in their thousands upon thousands swarmed on him, setting his skin on fire and turning his ears to flame. He breathed them in – he could taste the acidity. He was running with sweat and his lungs were labouring.

To his infinite relief, the plantation turned out to be narrow, soon giving way to a broad, grassy firebreak before mixed planting of conifers and hardwoods began. Julian stopped, mopped his brow to discourage the last of the midges and looked at his watch. They could surely not have climbed much higher or the man who had returned for some forgotten item could not have gone and returned in the time – unless he had laid it down somewhere short of the burial site and recovered it from there. That seemed unlikely. For a moment his heart sank. Could he be so wrong? Or had the woman at the inn overcooked the soup? Young Dean had been in the area, of that he was sure. But was Dean now sitting it out in some secure refuge? Was he, Julian, about to make an appalling ass of himself in the presence of senior police officers, with whom he would have to deal again during his career as a solicitor? Was he going to be unable to help Delia? He was prey to doubts similar to those that had beset Delia while she had followed the white van. For the briefest of moments he wondered whether Inspector Fauldhouse could be right and she had indeed murdered her brother.

Fifty paces along the firebreak to his right, a raggedness of the grass could be seen even from his low level. He walked in that direction. His spirits were divided. This was one occasion when he hated to be right. Like Grace, he had never met Dean Murray yet had developed a fondness for the mischievous, talented boy. But surplus earth had been scattered in the grass or tossed into the conifers. A slightly humped rectangle of disturbed ground was visible. Small clumps of grass and weeds had been replanted but the weeds, lacking water, had wilted. Grass was already regenerating from the buried roots and Julian guessed that within a fortnight of the next rain the soil would have settled and the grave would have become invisible.

He stood for a moment with his head lowered, which was all the respect that he could spare the time for. His moment of reverie was broken by the chirp of his mobile phone.

Dell was calling him. 'Two men just started up the hill, the way you went. At that distance I didn't get a very good look at them, but one of them looked pretty much like the man I picked up in the bucket of the digger. He looked much the way I imagine Satan in a bad mood might look.'

'They didn't see you?'

'I don't think so. They arrived from the other side and never looked this way. I ducked down.'

'Keep the phones connected,' Julian said, 'but we'll observe radio silence until we've something important to communicate.'

'Got you.'

Julian dropped his phone into his pocket and hurried towards the path by which he had arrived. He could hear them coming. But his footfalls were silent on the grass while the men were coming over much harder ground. By the sound of their approach, they had only just entered the path through the conifer plantation.

He turned back and crossed the firebreak. He had no intention of becoming involved in rough stuff. He could have hidden among the conifers, intending to join the path and slip away, but from stalking experience he knew that the spruce or fir branches would be impossible to pass in silence while wearing his waterproof jacket. He could have removed the jacket but the white shirt underneath would have shone through the trees like a beacon. The mixed plantation offered better prospects of hiding and flight than the unmixed conifers.

This phase of the planting had been carried out while sparing the best of the preexisting hardwoods. A large and spreading sycamore towered above the other trees. In its shade the other trees had been starved of sunlight. He made his way quickly to the trunk. Another lesson learned while stalking deer was that people and large mammals seldom look upwards. Sycamores are not usually well provided with foot and hand-holds among the lower branches, but although a single low limb had at some time been sawn off there was enough left to give him a start. A leap and a scramble and he was ten feet up and climbing. He was soon among foliage about thirty feet up, and although not perfectly screened he reckoned that this should be enough to preserve him from the casual upward glance. As the men emerged from the mouth of the path he wedged himself into a convenient crotch.

Two figures had appeared. There was no mistaking the menace in their attitudes. Each was carrying a section of silver birch log about the length and girth of a man's forearm, with one end shaped to make a handgrip. As a passing thought, the lawyer in him acknowledged that the weapons made sense. A section of log need only be tossed on to a handy bonfire to be beyond forensic study, but lacking an available bonfire several innocent explanations could be found for carrying a piece of log. Even more disturbingly, one of them was also carrying a spade.

One of the men he had already seen but only in the most adverse conditions, in almost complete darkness and while he was concussed. The other was easily eliminated, being smaller but thin and wiry. He was the one carrying the spade. Process of elimination, if nothing else, would have satisfied Julian that the other was his assailant of three days earlier. He was bulky enough to resemble the silhouette that Julian had seen against the sky, he looked strong enough to manhandle an unconscious man and he moved with a confidence that marked him as the leader. Even in repose his face had the downturned look of bad temper. With real anger superimposed, he did at least look, as Delia had suggested, like Satan in a bad mood. This then would be Cadiss while the first man, who carried the spade, must be Fergus Donelly.

Cadiss marched straight to the presumed grave site. Seeing it undisturbed, he took up his stance nearby and nodded to Donelly.

'Go ahead,' he said. 'Let's see if you're as good as you say you are.'

Donelly nodded in return and began to cast about. Julian was perturbed to see that he seemed well accustomed to reading traces on the ground. He moved like a forester or a gamekeeper, moving his head from side to side to catch the light reflected from a leaf or blade that had not yet returned from its trodden down position. Julian tried to make himself very small and to huddle into the crotch of the tree, then to still his movements and shade the white of his face, but these were futile measures. Donelly picked up his tracks through the grass almost immediately and followed them in the direction of the big sycamore. As soon as he saw where the tracks were leading, he looked up, craning this way and that to peer through the foliage. From feeling well hidden Julian felt dangerously exposed.

Evidently a man of few words, Donelly looked at Cadiss and pointed up with his birch club. Cadiss approached. He was looking directly at Julian.

Julian made a last attempt at reason. 'Do not do anything rash,' he said. 'They know where I've gone and why.'

The man with the spade, Donelly, said, 'The girl knows where you've gone. Amos is dealing with her now.' His voice was rasping.

It was not, after all, time for reasoning. The thought of Delia in the hands of the fat man set his blood hammering in his ears. The men were closing on his tree. Julian had not known that his brain could work so quickly. In the blinking of an eye he decided that Delia must wait just a little longer. She was tough, clever and ruthless.

First he must save himself. But the two men were between him and the track down to the scrapyard. The conifers on either side were thickly planted and well grown to about twice the height of a man – before he could crash a way through them, one of the men could be waiting for him on the other side.

Cadiss was looking up at him. His expression left Julian in no doubt as to who was to get the blame for the other's ride on the digger. 'You,' said Cadiss. 'You come down here.'

Julian gave a negative reply couched in terms that no lawyer should even know let alone use. His intention was to spur Cadiss into some rash act but it failed. Cadiss looked around and up the tree, evidently weighing up his chances of climbing up to Julian without being kicked in the head and deciding that they were not good. He weighed the club in his hand, but any attempt to throw it through the network of branches was forlorn and might be presenting Julian with a weapon.

'Go back to the car,' Cadiss told his henchman. 'Fetch your shotgun and a few cartridges. And hurry.' Donelly turned and plodded along the firebreak. 'Now are you coming down?' Cadiss asked Julian.

This was really serious. Drastic action was called for. Without answering, Julian descended a few feet. He took out his mobile phone. 'Any word from the police?' he asked it.

'Nothing yet.'

'Get on to them. Tell them that the body of Dean Murray is buried up here and that Cadiss, the guilty party, is threatening me.'

That was enough. Cadiss saw red. He hurled his club. It glanced off the trunk of the tree and struck Julian a glancing blow on the temple. Cadiss threw himself at the tree. As he was hauling himself on to the lowest, sawn-off, limb Julian descended by the two branches immediately below him. His timing was perfect. His heavy brogue, swung with all his muscle, caught Cadiss under the angle of the jaw. The man lost his grip and fell backwards. The thump on to hard ground drove the breath out of him.

Julian looked down for less than a second, but it was long enough for him to remember that he was sworn to uphold the law, and the law was clear. Cadiss was no longer a threat. But Julian had been knocked out, threatened with death and only saved by the courage and skill of a young New Zealand girl. Dean Murray, a gifted young man whose twist of humour might have led to higher things, had been led astray and then put down in a dispute over money. Julian had spent his adult life in the service of the law but now the law seemed inadequate. Once, he had comforted a client whose appeal had been thrown out by telling him of prison reforms, the comforts, the leisure, the television. A period of incarceration in those conditions might be enough retribution for a blow struck in a drunken rage. For Cadiss, however...

Julian explained it later to himself by arguing that he had been afraid of breaking his ankles if he came down on to the hard ground. Instead, he jumped down from a height on to the prone man's midriff.

When he recovered his balance he saw that Cadiss was rolled into a ball. His face was already turning blue and twisted into a shape barely human. If he did not get air soon he would be in great danger of brain damage, but to the brain of a man like Cadiss any change, Julian was sure, would be for the better. He turned away. He picked up the sycamore club and looked at the other man for a few long seconds. But his lust for real justice was satisfied. He turned away again and headed for the path through the conifers, bracing himself for a confrontation with the midges.

Eighteen

Delia sat with the engine running and watched Julian until he was out of sight. She had been nursing an idea. She did not mention it to Julian because the idea was extravagant, ridiculous, barely possible. It was a wild and desperate throw of the dice. But now she made up the mind. She would surely have time enough before the mobile phones were needed. In the grip of apprehension she could hear her own heart beating, yet she was smiling fondly. Julian had begun to have that effect on her.

She had spent her youth in the shadow of her father and then her brother, each determined to protect her not only from the ills of life but also from its delights. She had welcomed the approach of a respectable suitor as offering an escape from the sheep station where she had been regarded, she believed, as an inconvenient responsibility. Her heart had not been so engaged that the defection of the fiancé damaged it in any way. The death of Aloysius, while heart breaking at family level, had for a few moments offered escape, but the chill reality of life without the embrace of family protection had struck home immediately.

Julian had come galloping to the rescue like a knight in only slightly tarnished armour. From their first meeting she had recognized in him a fellow spirit, one who would always be there to offer comfort or help. With the passing days she had also recognized a keen intelligence and a brave determination. He was a rock, a sturdy prop, increasingly directing his support towards Delia Barrow in particular rather than the world in general. They had so much in common and yet their differences meshed together like ... she discarded the thought of the two halves of a broken plate. That simile suggested a disaster. She preferred to think of two cogs in a machine. He had become so much a part of her life that she could no longer imagine life without him.

The number answered. She spoke quickly for less than a minute and then cleared the line.

Julian was, she realized, shy with women. On occasions he had seemed to be on the verge of a word or a gesture that might have been aimed towards a more amorous relationship, but each time he had retreated. At first she had been hurt; later she realized that his reserve stemmed from fear of rejection, or of laying himself open to ridicule or worse if he failed to interpret correctly that rejection. A lawyer must have observed occasions when a man had strayed over the line dividing courtship from harassment, assault or stalking. In her half-waking moments she had decided, correctly, that at some time a woman had rejected his advances cruelly, exposing him to the derision of his acquaintances. Delia would very much have liked to scratch that offender's face off. There was an obvious cure for the inhibitions that beset Julian and when she felt that the moment was ripe, despite the slenderness of her own experience, she would not hesitate to offer it; but she would much prefer that he cured himself, using her as the medicine. Her experience of matters amorous might be slight – only the now half-forgotten fiancé had penetrated her defences – but she had every woman's instinctive knowledge of how to make best use of her allure.

He was out of sight now, but still she mused. She was in no doubt that her future was twined with his. More and more the sight or sound of him, the very thought of him in his absence, made her go, quite literally, 'weak at the knees'. A solicitor's wife instead of a sheep-farmer's sister. For the first time ever, she considered herself in the role of a possible mother.

She was so rapt in her dream that she hardly noticed the two men who approached through the scattered trees beyond the scrapyard and turned up the path that Julian had followed. She used the phone to warn him. With that warning, surely he would be able to cope. But suppose he was rash and decided to confront the men. Suppose ... But her mind refused to contemplate any outcome but living happily-ever-after. She let her dream return, interrupted only by Julian's enquiry as to whether the police had arrived.

A family would be a burden and a responsibility. She had had little to do with children. Those belonging to the neighbours in New Zealand had been physically distant

276

and quite without relevance to her own life. Those that she had passed in the street or seen running loose in an airport had been lacking in charm, but just recently they had begun to exert some sort of siren call. She had not reached the stage of peering into other people's prams, but if the children were Julian's children, that would be altogether different. In the process of continuing the human race Julian, surely, would manage to sire little people with charisma, tact, strength of character – people, in fact, very much like himself. Somebody had told her that the first twenty years were the worst.

In her reverie, miniatures of Julian showered affection on her or came running to her side for reassurance or comfort. She was jerked back to reality and her heart set pounding by a big shadow between her window and the fence and a hand jerking at the door. It belonged to the barrel-shaped proprietor of the yard. But she had locked the doors as Julian had told her. Her heart, still pounding, leaped into her mouth as his hand, hairy and rimed with dirt, was forced in at the narrow opening of the window and groped for the door lock.

Her first impulse was to freeze but a more

mature thought told her that this would not be a good moment for inertia. Life on the sheep station had confronted her with occasional emergencies and she had learned to think quickly and to react on the instant. The window was only open a matter of a few inches and the controls were just under her hand rather than his. She found the right switch and rocked it in the right direction at the first try. With the car's engine running, the glass slid up the available inch. It clamped his wrist in a vice-like grip and stopped.

Through the window, they glared at each other. His nose was flattened against the glass, giving him the look of a big ape.

The man had evidently been doing some minor carpentry job, because in his other hand he had a thin batten of rough wood. He pushed it in through the window. It hit the side of her nose. He stooped again to look in at her. 'Open up,' he said, 'or I'll poke your eye out.' He jabbed.

Delia grabbed the stick and twisted. There was a knot near his hand and the stick broke, leaving him with a few inches of timber in his hand and a large splinter lodged under his thumbnail. He spluttered with frustration, called her a very rude word and tried to extract the splinter, using his teeth.

Delia already had the car in 'D'. She lifted her foot off the brake and touched the throttle. The car jerked forward. It was already parked on a line converging with the fence. Perforce the man moved with it, stumbling sideways and swearing as he went. He was soon pressed up against the sheep-mesh and then rolled along it. The car shook, the fence twanged and his arm was twisted into an impossible shape. If the bone was not broken the shoulder was surely dislocated. The car was braked to a halt by the resistance of his body. The man was now facing the fence, jammed hard against it with his arm twisted behind him. She expected him to roar with pain. His face was above her head and turned away from her but such sound of his voice as reached her suggested that his jaw was clenched tight.

Her experiences on the sheep station had taught her to keep her head in a crisis. Now she surprised herself by thinking with a clarity that seemed new to her. She put her hand down and pressed home the cigar lighter. She might wish to ask some question and his fingertips were conveniently placed.

'What did you call me?' she asked him.

'Say it again.'

The air was being squeezed out of his lungs but he managed to snatch a quick breath. 'You bitch,' he ground out, 'I'm going to have you before this is over.'

'You are, are you?' she said grimly.

'Yes I bloody am. And you needn't look for your fancy man to come and save you.' His voice came in short gasps as he struggled for one breath at a time. 'There's two very hard men dealing with him this minute and when they've finished with him they'll be down here to deal with you.'

'Who will?'

'*They* will.'

'Who's they? I mean, who are they?'

The man drew several breaths as deep as he could manage. 'I'm not telling you that. Bugger off.'

The cigar lighter popped out. She took it up. 'Who?' she repeated.

'You'll know soon enough when they –'

Delia had had enough and she was sure that time was short. She touched the glowing lighter to his thumbnail. 'Cadiss and Donelly,' he shouted.

Delia touched the throttle again and then pulled on the handbrake. Leaving the car still ticking over, Delia lifted her feet over the levers, slid across the passenger seat and unlocked the doors. Before quitting the car she returned the cigar lighter tidily to its socket. She was a very tidy person.

She limped quickly along the fence and in at the gate. Her impulse was to go to Julian's aid, but she had more faith in his ability to cope than in her own ability to hurry uphill or to deal with the two hard men if she arrived on a scene of roughhouse. Even so ... this man was not going anywhere and he might have a use as a hostage. She could see a faint possibility that the two hard men might value her prisoner's life above Julian's.

The yard was untidy to a degree that offended her womanly soul. Tools lay where they had last been used. She looked them over. Most of them were familiar to her from her days on the sheep station. All the while the man's gasping voice pursued her. He began with a catalogue of what he would do to her, and it did not make pretty listening. Soon it seemed to dawn on him that he was not ingratiating himself with somebody who had the power to maim him. From threatening he went to arguing, justifying and finally pleading. She ignored every word of it. She was not looking for any particular tool but she would know it when she saw it.

Almost anything sharp would have done but soon she came across a Stihlsaw – a two-stroke motor powering a high-speed cutting disk impregnated with diamond dust. It lay beside a half-dismantled Transit van. Life on the sheep station had given her a familiarity with power tools. She could feel faint warmth from the motor. 'You are, are you?' she repeated.

The man's eyes popped. 'What're you do-ing?'

He was pressed so hard against the fence that areas of fat the size of a handprint bulg-ed through the mesh. She pulled the starter-cord. The motor whirred but failed to catch. 'I'm going to cut off anything this side of the wires,' she said.

The man tried to pull away but he had no space to move. The car door, in particular, was ramming his bottom towards the fence so that the fat of his belly made quilt-like patterns. Delia pulled the cord again. The motor whirred, coughed twice but stopped.

'You can't,' he squealed.

'Watch me,' she said. 'You can tell me something.'

'Tell you what?'

'Those bricks blocking the doorway. Are they solid tin?'

'No. 'Course they're not.'

Delia swung away. She limped to the doorway and gave the cord another pull. This time the little motor leaped into life. When she touched the throttle the tool leaped in her hand and the disk span into a blur. She applied the disk to the corner of one of the blocks and a bright silver wound showed through. She released the throttle and with the machine ticking over she walked back to the fence.

'You've had your one lie,' she said. 'Now tell the truth. Is Dean Murray's body buried up there?'

He hesitated. She came closer and touched the throttle. At the sudden blast of sound his nerve broke. 'Yes,' he shouted.

'Who killed him?'

Again the hesitation, again the blast of sound. 'I don't know. I wasn't there.'

'You know all right.' She moved the Stihl-saw closer. It caught a button on the man's dungarees. The button whirred away and clinked down among the scrap metal, leaving a rip in the cloth not far from the bulge

283

made by his genitalia.

The close proximity of mutilation was enough to break his nerve. 'All right. I do know. I wasn't there but I heard them talk.' The fat man's voice had gone up to a squeak of terror. Delia with her anger showing was a fearsome sight. 'It was the big one. The plumber.'

'What's his name?'

'Cadiss.'

'That's enough,' said a deep voice. Inspector Welles came through the gate and relieved her of the Stihlsaw – to her relief, because its considerable weight was an almost impossible burden for a woman with part-healed damage to one arm and one leg, and when push came to shove she had not been at all sure that she could bring herself to cut bits off another ostensibly human being in not very hot blood. 'He's told me what I'm going to have to prove by other means,' he said. 'Any more coercion and whatever evidence is still to be gathered will never be admissible. I suggest to you that your recent exchange never happened.' He was looking into her eyes and his deep voice was almost hypnotically persuasive. 'I certainly didn't hear it. Now back the car and we'll get him collected by ambulance.'

Julian had said that he would take his own chances. But it dawned on her that she had been rather neglecting her side of the partnership. 'But Julian ... Mr Custer...'

'He's all right. I've just spoken to him on his phone. He's just as concerned about you.'

Seconds later Julian came down the track, running. From higher up, he had heard the song of the Stihlsaw and seen the car in police livery with two officers in uniform and another figure in plain clothes. When he could be sure that everything was under control he slowed, panting, and leaned against the mesh until he had recovered his breath. 'I can show you what seems to be a grave,' he said. 'Or tell you exactly where to find it. And the guilty man is still up there. I may have damaged him but he was coming after me at the time. The other one, Donelly, could be back at any moment. Cadiss sent him to fetch his shotgun.'

Delia's stomach gave a lurch when she saw the blood on his head. She got into the car and scrambled over the gear and handbrake levers again. Julian followed her. She took stock of the situation. It was obvious that reversing might only worsen the fat man's injuries. The law might disapprove. 'If I back the car,' she told the inspector, 'it'll probably tear his arm off.'

'You could be right.' Inspector Welles was still holding the Stihlsaw. He spoke to the fat man, who was still bulging through the mesh of the fence. 'In front of witnesses,' he said, 'I want your permission to cut the wire.' He turned to the two men with him. 'You two, relieve Mr Custer of that club and go to meet Donelly. Persuade him to give up his shotgun. If he turns awkward, come back for me.'

Delia lowered the driver's window and the fat man's arm flopped down sickeningly. He groaned and seemed ready to faint.

'You're going to have your hands full for the next few hours,' Delia told the inspector. 'Mr Custer needs attention. Let him tell you where to find the grave. We'll wait for you at the Balnagairn Inn. The evidence you need to tie it all together is waiting for you there.'

The inspector looked at her steadily. 'Very well,' he said at last. 'Be there.' He lost interest in mere witnesses and used his radio to call for backup and an ambulance.

Nineteen

The few minutes of travelling between the scrapyard and the inn were passed in silence except for the hum of the car. Events were too big and too recent for easy words. Della used her free hand to rub the back of Julian's hand before returning it hastily to the wheel. As she parked in front of the inn she said, 'Does this put me in the clear now?'

Julian made a face. 'It's touch and go,' he said. 'On the evidence, a court might decide that Dean Murray caused the accident that killed your brother and was murdered by the other two in the course of a quarrel over money and to prevent him drawing attention to their theft of the tin. Frankly, I wouldn't expect it to get as far as a court anyway. The police won't pursue it and if they did the procurator fiscal would probably throw it out. And if the fiscal went mad and decided

287

to proceed the sheriff would stop it at the preliminary hearing. What'll probably happen is that the sheriff will hold an inquiry and the jury will bring in a verdict of murder. They don't usually point to the guilty party and in this instance I don't see them doing so. My guess is that your worries may soon be over as far as the danger of prosecution. But clearing your name is another matter. If the unpleasant Mr Maclure makes enough allegations and enough supporting evidence gets fabricated, you might be tainted forever with suspicion in the public mind. I just wish that I could clear your name. In other words, I'd like proof of innocence, not absence of proof of guilt. You follow me?'

'I follow you.' They sat in silence for another minute. 'Your head needs attention,' Delia said suddenly. 'Let's go in.'

'There's blood on your face too.'

'He jabbed at me with a stick, but I reckon I got rather more than my due revenge, rolling him along the wire.' She chuckled but, looking at her, Julian saw that she was laughing through tears. 'And I scared him out of his wits when I took the power-saw to him. We'll get cleaned up inside.'

The blonde woman met them in the porch, beside the sculpture that still bore Dean Murray's handiwork. She drew in her breath when she saw the blood on Julian's face and the slight smear on Delia's nose.

'Don't worry,' Delia told her, putting an arm around the older woman's shoulders. 'These are only scratches. Both of those men that you were afraid of are being hunted by the police this minute. The one who really scared you is injured and I should think he's already in custody. The police will soon be here to take your statement. Your part's almost over except to give the evidence that will finally sink them.'

The woman leaned back against the wall as though her knees were failing her. 'God, I hope so! After I've given my statement I'll take refuge with my cousins a long way away from here until those buggers come up for trial. And then I'll look them in the eye from the witness stand and we'll see who's afraid. Was I right? Did they kill that laddie?'

'I'm afraid so,' Julian said. 'I've just found where they buried him. And I set the police on the trail. It's a sad story and I'm afraid that it may be up to me to go and break it to his parents. I'm not looking forward to that.'

'If you like, I'll come with you,' Dell offered.

He gave her a quick and clumsy hug. 'I'd appreciate that.'

'It's settled, then. And now, can we use the toilet to clean ourselves up? Could you perhaps give us the use of a private bathroom?'

Without a pause the landlady straightened up and switched into business mode. 'Bedroom Number One has an *en suite* bathroom. Come in and I'll give you the key and some towels.'

Tenderly, they cleaned each other up in the bathroom. Delia's scratch was too superficial to require more than a gentle wash. She had borrowed scissors and a plaster from the blonde woman. She clipped the hair away from the wound on Julian's head and decided that it did not need stitches. 'You still have a lump left from the last time you were swatted with a tree-limb,' she told him. 'You'd have felt it if this had caught you in the same place.'

'I felt it anyway,' he said. 'And I felt that,' he added as she applied the plaster.

'I'd have been worried if you hadn't. I had to patch up enough knocks and injuries back in New Zealand, what with people getting careless with tools or falling off horses. One thing I learned was that wounds are supposed to hurt. If they don't, there's nerve damage.'

When they were both clean and as tidy as they could manage, they found that they were in a vacuum. There was little left to say and nothing to do. They adjourned into the bedroom. The only chair was a hard, upright chair. They took seats on the bed, side by side. The cheerful noises from the bar came up to them but they had no spirit left for company.

'What was it that you didn't want the nurse to tell me?' Julian asked her out of the blue. Delia was silent. He turned to look at her. She had blushed scarlet. 'Well, tell me,' he said.

'There's no way of saying it that doesn't make me sound like an idiot,' she muttered.

He took her hand and resisted her feeble efforts to pull it away. 'But I know that you're not an idiot,' he assured her. 'I've told you often enough that I think you're clever. I probably said brilliant and I meant it.'

She looked away. 'I'd appreciate that more if you hadn't also told me that I'm beautiful. That doesn't show you as a very truthful person.'

Julian's muscles were protesting that they were not accustomed to hurrying uphill or to running away from pursuing murderers. Sitting upright on a soft bed with the back unsupported puts a lot of strain on certain muscles. He was stiffening up. He turned to lie flat on the bed with Delia sitting beside him. It had been dawning on him that her mind was closely attuned to his but that, although her body was fit and muscled from her life in New Zealand, it was also soft and rounded. 'To me,' he said thoughtfully, 'you are beautiful. Beautiful all over. Remember, I've seen you getting out of the shower.' He thought that the time might be ripe for telling her that she had the world's most beautiful bottom, and then decided against it. Compliments are not always taken in the spirit in which they were given. 'Your figure is truly lovely and your face, when nobody is accusing you of murdering anybody, looks as though you're sure that something marvellous is about to happen. It's looking a bit that way just now. But what do I know? I don't think that Madonna is beautiful. When you take trouble, you're beautiful to me. But I rather prefer you when you're just yourself with your hair loose. You have a lovely skin. I could look into your eyes and...'

She had turned back and lowered her face. He found himself looking into her eyes. After some seconds, rather than allow the conversation to peter out altogether, she closed them. 'Really?' she said.

'Really. And then there's your mouth. So many women's faces are spoiled by their mouths, but yours is perfection. Full lips but not too full and always looking ready to smile. And I've been dreaming about your figure. Now will you tell me?'

Delia opened her eyes and came back to the here and now. 'Tell you what?'

'What it was that you wouldn't let the nurse tell me.'

She sighed. 'If you promise not to think that I'm an idiot, all right. You see, I've spent so much of my life on a sheep station. I can shear a sheep. I can ride a horse or a motorbike, use a shotgun or a rifle, chop logs or build a fence. I've had to learn to beat off any man that tries to grab me – my father and my brother made sure of that. But my mother died a long time ago, so what I've never learned are the girly things.'

This line of thought was entirely fresh and

strange to Julian. 'I never thought that they had to be learned. I mean, a girl is a girl and you're a girl. So when it comes to attracting me you're already most of the way there.'

'Am I really? You see, I wanted you to think of me as a girl, not as one of the blokes who goes around beating up hard men.'

'When a hard man has dropped me down a hole and is about to fill it in on top of me, you're welcome to intervene. Believe me, you won't attract me any less.'

Dell made an indignant face, half laughing. 'There you go again. You never come out and say that I attract you, only oblique things like that I wouldn't attract you any less. What's that supposed to mean? I'm probably not being girlish, saying any of this, but I can't help it while I think we both know that there's a hell of a lot going on between us that never gets said aloud and you won't utter a damn word. Or am I wrong?'

'No, you're not wrong.'

'Do I really attract you?' she asked in a very small voice.

'You must know that you attract the hell out of me,' he said.

But still he just lay there. He was holding on tight to her hand, but that was not enough. She sighed. She was throwing away the girlishness that should have been her only weapon, but there is such a thing as being too damn gentlemanly. Perhaps he would only want her for a pal. 'Then why won't you bloody well say so? Why do I have to say it for you? You're very shy of women, aren't you?' she said. 'Why is that?'

He looked away but his grip on her hand tightened. He pulled her towards him. 'That was four questions on the trot and you didn't wait for me to answer any one of them. You were honest with me so I'll be honest with you. I think it stems from an incident years ago, when I was a first-year student. I don't suppose you'll believe this. You'll think I was a bloody fool.'

'I promise I won't,' she said. 'And I always keep my promises.'

'We'll see. When I was a first-year student I had a fancy for a girl in my year. She was pretty and she knew it. I saw her later, once, without her makeup and she was nothing special so it must have just been cleverness. Thinking it over since, I'm still sure that she gave me some very definite come-on signals and the whole thing was a nasty trick for her own amusement or to boost her ego. I was young and shy but I knew what I wanted and she convinced me that she wanted it too. The long and short of it is that I tried it on, she smacked my face and for the rest of our time at university she was telling everybody a very lopsided version of the story. It didn't do me any harm with the men students.'

Della was not in the least gratified that her guess had been so close to the mark. 'That's very close to what I already suspected. I would have thought that some of the girls would still have chased after you.'

'Looking back, I think that some of them did, but they were a little too subtle and I was a great deal too young and stupid and timid to be caught again.'

'And you still are?'

'Perhaps, except that I'm not young any more. And I'm not totally innocent. I've had offers. Some of them were so blatant that not even I could mistake them. I told you that you wouldn't believe it.'

Delia smiled secretly but then made up her mind. 'I believe that all right.' It was now or never. 'You don't have to do anything about it if you don't want to,' she said hoarsely. 'But I promise that I wouldn't reject you. And I certainly wouldn't tell. I wouldn't have to. People would know because I would be going around with such a smile on my face. Listen, I'll make it easy for you. I'll tell you the answer first. It's *Yes*. Now you ask me if I love you.'

Her coat had been thrown over the foot of the bed. Before he could answer, her mobile phone in the pocket began to ring. By slow stages, she had inserted herself into his arms but now she struggled to reach her phone. 'I'm not rejecting you,' she said. I'm not. It's just that I think this is the answer to a call I made while I was waiting in the car and you were on your way up the hill.'

'You were supposed to be keeping the phone free for my message.'

'It was before you could possibly have reached the top.'

He relaxed his grip slightly and she managed to reach her phone. She keyed in and listened. The caller's voice was female. He could only make out the occasional word but he saw that smile breaking out again. When she broke the connection, she said, 'My phone call was to Mrs Welles. You see, I remembered that in New Zealand, sometimes for quite lengthy periods, the wives of policemen knew or could find out almost anything. Men talk to their wives more than they realize. They need somebody they can talk to, get rid of the worries, you know what I mean?'

'Lord, yes!'

'Well, that's how it was. And it's a recognized fact that the wisdom of a group is always more than that of the individuals.'

'I've noticed the same thing,' Julian said. 'A group seems to act like a simple computer.'

'Right. And wives talk to each other. While you were looking up our route on the road atlas, I talked with Mrs Welles and we got on very well. What's more, she wasn't altogether ignorant about what we were trying to do. So I thought it was worth consulting her about who's been making up stories about me. She spoke to some other policemen's wives. When she called me back just now, she had a lot to tell me.

'For a start, I'd been wondering whether Inspector Fauldhouse was quite as incorruptible as he would want us to believe. To be frank, and very, very strictly between ourselves, I could afford to offer him one hell of a bribe now.'

Julian jumped and tried to sit up but the effort was too great. He sounded as if for two pins he would be pacing the room while wringing his hands and groaning. In the momentary silence a sudden burst of laughter from the bar beneath them sounded very loud. 'My God!' Julian exclaimed. 'You didn't suggest any such thing?'

'No, I didn't. I'm not altogether an idiot, whatever you think. As it turns out, she was able to tell me that his reputation inside the Force is for being a bit dim and pig-headed but straight. What she did find out for me is that he asked Strathclyde for help in investigating my cousins and the nasty Mr Maclure. Not for my sake, I'm damn sure, but in the hope of busting open my version of things. I'm not putting this very well,' she added.

'I understand you. I may not like it, but I understand it.'

'You can smack my bottom later.'

'I may take you up on your kind invitation. Or I may not. So what did he find out?'

Delia paused for a second, her attention caught by their exchange. 'Not what he wanted to find out,' she said. 'Strathclyde Police only took minutes to tell him that Mr Maclure lives next door but one to my cousins. That's as far as it's gone, but she'll phone me again as soon as she hears of any more developments.'

Julian heaved a sigh of undiluted happiness. 'That was what we needed to hear. The implication, that there was a conspiracy to edge you out of your inheritance, is just as strong as any of the suspicions being raised against you. It opens up a crack in the allegations. If we have to, we can drive in a wedge to force the whole conspiracy apart. If necessary, you can well afford to put private detectives on to tracing the source of every allegation, but I don't think it'll be necessary.'

'Good,' said Delia. 'Now ask me.'

'Ask you what?'

She gave him a small shake. 'You're not listening to the really important things,' she said severely. 'Ask me if I love you.'

He turned to face her. Their noses were almost touching. She moved in closer. Her breath tickled his nose. The tip of a tongue coaxed his lips apart. She still had his hand and she moved it to where she desired it.

Two minutes later she knew the fullest meaning of the expression about having a tiger by the tail. She had no say whatever in what was to follow. In his relief he was ready to appreciate what he held in his arms. More than that, she had turned him into a wild beast. She was kissed and fondled until she thought that, like some cartoon character, steam must be coming out of her ears. She was respectfully grabbed, picked up, turned round, stripped, rolled over, kissed and fondled some more. At some point he too seemed to have shed his clothes, but whether he or she had pulled them off she had no idea. She was more than ready. She was laid back, folded in half and ravished mercilessly, time and again. She could not protest because her mouth was full of his tongue.

It was wonderful. It went beyond even her wildest dreams without stepping over the boundaries of her acceptance. So this, she thought, was both happiness and pleasure and she had never known either.

Only later did they realize that all sound from the bar downstairs had ceased.